A Tiara of
Emerald Thorns

A Tiara of Emerald Thorns

By
Rebecca Cavanaugh

ISBN: 978-1-7369732-0-2 (paperback)
ISBN: 978-1-7369732-1-9 (ebook)

Dedicated To:
My Parents, Brother, Friends, Family and Mentors.
Thank you for believing in Me.

In Memory Of:
Richard Cavanaugh

Contents

Dear Reader,

The planet of Aquamarine is a mostly uninhabited planet. This is due to the many mountains and forested areas leaving very few places for major settlements to be established. The story that is about to transpire only takes place in the most populated parts of the planet. Here there was an immense valley, only disrupted by small hills and a river, that would allow for groups of Aquamarinian people to settle and for a major city to grow.

This relatively small planet does have towns and villages by the names of Touringrin, Mourif, Coarif, and Ferrenlin. These are the largest of the smaller settlements that are not mentioned in the story; others are less known, and their names seem to change every time one asks about them. These places are settled near lakes and mountain rivers that are scattered around Aquamarine. The laws of Aquamarine do apply to all Aquamarinian subjects, but these places are mostly left alone.

It should be noted that the Forests of Magus and Promise merge at some point beyond the Mountains of Treachery to become the Forest of Veteris Ferigan Magus. This knowledge escapes the current ruler of the planet, but the fact remains that this forest covers most of the planet. The rest of the areas that have gone unmentioned include small rivers and ponds that are known by name only to those who live there.

While these people and places usually go unaffected by events of their planet's political center, they are just as important. For their lives, too, hang in the balance of what is about to take place...

CHAPTER 1

Revelation

"*I*t sure is a long way down," Rose said as she looked at the ground from the plane that she was about to jump out of. Rose Heartington was a good-looking young woman with long, straight black hair, pale skin, and electric-green eyes. She was wearing her favorite pair of high-heel boots and was seriously considering hitting her boyfriend, James Tungston, as hard as she could for convincing her to do this.

"Rose, really, it isn't that hard, and trust me, you're going to love it," he said with that beautiful smile that got her every time. He had soft, brown, wavy hair, a perfect smile, and incredibly beautiful brown eyes. "You look like you're about to beat me up."

"That's because I am, and believe me when I say that I am never going to let you convince me to do something like this again!" Then, thinking about how great he looked when the sun hit him like that, she followed the instructor that she had for what felt like only a few days, knowing that it had been weeks, out of the plane. The feeling was like nothing she had ever experienced, and it was even more incredible to watch James.

"That was absolutely amazing! I can't believe that I just did that. Words can't even begin to describe what I am feeling right now." And she still couldn't believe how lucky she was to have met him...

Three years later...

Rose is running the little florist shop left to her by her late father and has long forgotten that summer when she was eighteen. Her life is normal, and she feels perfectly content with that fact. With her favorite pair of boots clipping on the shop's stone floor, she goes to the counter to answer the telephone that is ringing.

"Rose's Rosary, this is Rose speaking. How may I help you?"

"Hey, Rose, it's James," said the voice that she knew only too well. "Are you in a place where you can talk freely?" Why does he sound so nervous? And what does he mean by can you speak freely?

"James, what is it? And why do you sound out of breath?" she asked as she took the phone into the back room. There was a moment's hesitation and a little more heavy breathing. "James, I am waiting for your answer, and I really don't have all day. I have three huge orders, and they are needed in four hours." Still silence, minus the heavy breathing.

"Rose," he paused, "they're coming to get you. You have to meet me at the end of the street, and there is no time to explain." Rose was so confused and annoyed that she wanted to hit him. He was being so secretive, and she was tired of it. She had left him when she had found out that he was different from most people, which she still didn't entirely believe, and she was in no mood to deal with his lies.

"James, if you can remember anything, you'll remember that the reason we haven't spoken is because you pushed me away with that ridiculous story you invented. Furthermore, you seem to think that there is another thing out to get me, which is just your way of getting back with me, I imagine." She said the last bit slowly, for it sounded as if someone had entered her shop. And what was even stranger, they seemed to have locked the door behind them. "James, I'll have to call you back. There's someone here."

"Rose, wait, don't—" she hung up, cutting him off midsentence. There were hushed voices in the background; the people were moving around.

One of the voices, a man's, spoke. "She has to be in here somewhere. The sign on the door said 'Open.'" His voice was followed by a female's, and while Rose noticed his was slightly gruff, hers was almost musical.

"Liam, you know darn well that it was James Tungsten that overheard us, and he probably rushed to tell her someone was after her." The young woman had called the man "Liam," and for some reason that name seemed familiar to her.

The man started to speak again. "Aphra Draughtningr, whatever James told her she is unlikely to believe, and you forget—if he hadn't found her for us, we wouldn't be here. So let's get her and get out of here before she tries to run." After he spoke the talking ceased.

Rose's heart was ramming against her ribcage, and as she slowly backed away, she felt herself panic and turn quickly around. She almost swore as she tripped over a decorative pot. It was decorated with a pattern resembling emerald-tinted thorns that she, up until that point at least, had always loved. The people in the other room burst through the door, and before Rose climbed out of the window that led to the alley, she saw two people who were almost godlike in their looks. Letting out a high-pitched scream, she began running for her life.

Somewhere behind her she heard the man yell, "Stop that woman!"

Soon Rose had to stop because of a stitch in her chest, and while breathing very quickly, she suddenly noticed that her feet had carried her within only fifty feet of the corner that James had said he would meet her at. Thinking that perhaps he was her only hope, she ran toward it. Avoiding vehicles and not even bothering with the crosswalk, Rose finally reached the corner only to find it completely James-less. Then, when she thought with horror, that things couldn't possibly get any worse, she heard a voice calling her name.

"Rose!" I know that voice, she thought, her heart taking a leap. "Rose, over here!" Rose turned and saw James. He was on the opposite corner of the street that she was on.

"James, why are there people chasing me!" He looked at her with sad eyes, and then they filled with fear.

"Rose, hurry over here! They're coming—you have to get to me before they get you!" His voice was so panic stricken that it seemed to belong to someone else. That's when Rose noticed someone move very suddenly behind him.

"James, behind you!" she screamed, and as he turned around, another pale-faced individual began to wrestle him to the ground. Each blow seemed to root Rose to the spot, and before she had a second's warning, two strong arms grabbed her around the waist.

"Let me go!" she screamed, hitting the individual lugging her into an alley and off of the sidewalk. "I said, release me! What part of *put me down* don't you understand!"

"Ooo, she is feisty," said the silky, musical voice that she remembered from her shop. "You know, I think our father was right about her, don't you, Liam?"

There was a short, kind of determined laugh coming from the man lugging her. Rose tried to struggle free, but when she began to think she had made some progress, she felt the arms grow tighter around her. Suddenly she saw something rather strange: there was a secret door in the wall, and as they approached it, it slowly came into focus, like a camera lens. Just as the door came into focus, Rose was placed down. Rose kicked the man.

"Ow! Aphra, get her before she gets away!" yelled Liam.

"No problem," and with an incredible burst of speed, she stood in front of Rose.

Too filled with shock, Rose only had enough time to slow down before ramming into Aphra. "Let me go! You know that what you are doing is considered kidnap here, and I would appreciate you letting me go!" It wasn't until now, however, that Rose got a good look at her captors. Liam was tall and broad, pale, with electric-blue eyes and wavy golden hair. The young woman, Aphra, was thin with the same electric-blue eyes with long, white-blond hair. She was also as pale as Liam, and they were both extremely beautiful.

"Please let me go. I have nothing to offer you. I don't even know you, so please, please just let me go." It was as she said this last sentence that Liam came slowly toward her, with Aphra right behind him.

"Number one, Rose, you do have something to offer us; you just don't know what it is. Number two, while you may not know us, we, along with our race, know you and have known you since you were a small child. Number three, we are not going to let you go after everything we had to go through to get you. Lastly, your friend James tried to stop our world from being put right by hiding you, after it was his job three years ago to bring you back to your people."

Suddenly Rose realized how close Liam was to her, and as she was about to move away, a smell, so sweet it made her dizzy, reached her nose. She felt woozy and faint, and she caught a glimpse of an uncorked bottle that Aphra was holding. As if he knew what was about to happen, Liam caught her just as she passed out.

CHAPTER 2

The Planet of Aquamarine

"Where am I?" groaned Rose as she took in her surroundings. The wildlife around her was like nothing that she had ever seen. Each plant looked as if it were alive, with colors so vibrant that it almost hurt to look at them. Along with the spectacular display of scenery was the room she was in. It was huge, and the paintings that covered the walls seemed to display the same object, except in different variations. It was what seemed to be an emerald tiara that was in the shape of rose thorns. While it was clear what it was, every painting, sketch, and drawing was a different theory, as if it had never been seen before.

"I must be dreaming, because the flowers here resemble the colors of jewels, and the room I am in is trimmed with gold." As she slowly got off of the bed she had been placed on, she began to admire the only piece of artwork that was not of the thorny tiara. It was the length of the room and seemed to be telling a story. Rose approached what seemed to be the beginning.

At the beginning, the land and people seemed happy and joyous, but as the painting got toward the middle of the room, things began to change. A great battle took place, and the leader of what was being portrayed as the invading side was shown killing what seemed to be the king. The next scene was showing the new regime, with the murderous leader in command with a very sinister-looking man standing just to his right. Just before the painting ended, it showed the secret celebration of the birth of a new baby girl and showed her being hidden on...

Rose stopped, not believing what was being displayed before her. The child that made so many people rejoice was placed on another *planet*. Not just any planet either: Earth. Then she found herself before what seemed to be the oldest of the thorny tiara paintings.

"And here I was thinking that people portrayed strange stories where I came from." But was it a story? she wondered. Was this a people's past, and what did the thorny tiara and that little girl have in common?

"Are you OK?" said the voice which she had wished never to hear again. "I hope that you will be willing to hear my side of the story, Rose."

"James?!" With thoughts streaming through her mind, some that were not exactly the nicest she could be thinking, she looked around to see where he was. Finally she spotted him in a shaded corner near an emerald-green rose bush.

"You sound and look as though you are about to hit me," he said with a little bit of humor that seemed to be deeply hidden in his voice and his past. "I must say that the years seem to have been good to you."

"Thanks," she replied, "and if the truth be told, for conversation's sake, you haven't changed much either." Then she turned back to the painting, giving him the cold shoulder.

"It's a sad story, isn't it?" he said to her, just barely catching her eye. "I used to think that this painting was just a story told to make people like me behave, but there came a point that led me to realize that there was way too much truth in it to just be a story."

"Come on, James, you expect me to believe that this painting represents an actual event!" Rose said sarcastically and in an unconvinced manner, "that I am on a completely different planet! You forget that I am no longer enamored with you." Even if you are still just as gorgeous as you were three years ago, she thought.

"The only thing I forgot was how quickly you could talk back," he remarked with a small smile, "and yes, I have noticed a change in you, which doesn't include, by the way, your favorite boots." Looking at her shocked and disgusted face made him laugh. "In all seriousness though, Rose, this story has everything to do with you and is the very reason that Liam and Aphra brought you to my house on our planet of Aquamarine."

"James, this is exactly why I left you in the first place. Do you really think that I believe tha—" James cut her off.

"Rose, then can you explain the strange wildlife!" he hollered at her. "Do you honestly think that you are still on the planet that you consider your home?"

"And what do you mean by 'consider'!" Rose retaliated, "Earth is my home. I have lived there my entire life! As for this plant life, I'll admit that it is a bit unusual!"

"Rose, you may have lived on Earth, but you weren't born there," he screamed back, his face getting blotchy, "you were born here, and that's why our people have been looking for you!" James stopped to catch his breath and what Rose assumed to be his temper. "Rose, I am sorry if you don't believe me, but this is where you are from." He seemed to desperately want her to believe him.

"James, you forget that you made up a huge story about who you were, where you came from, and what life was like there." Rose, while trying to keep her calm, continued, "You told me that where you were from, a creature was matched to your personality and that it chose you. That swords had names, and jewels came from rare plants. It broke my heart to hear what you told me because I felt that you were pushing me away." James hadn't interrupted her, and that was a sign that the truth meant something to him.

"Rose, I wasn't pushing you away," he explained, "I wanted nothing more than to be with you, and I couldn't with a lie hanging over my head, which is why I told you the truth." He waited for her to interrupt, and when she didn't he continued, "The whole truth is that I was sent to find you and bring you back, but I fell in love with you, and I couldn't justify lying to you anymore. Then when I told you the truth, you got all angry with me. I tried to find you, and when I failed, I came back here and said that I had never found you."

"Why did you lie?" Rose asked him with nothing short of venom in her voice.

"I didn't want those who were supposed to retrieve you if you refused to come with me to go after you." He stopped and looked at her as if what he was about to tell her next was his biggest mistake. "But I had kept a picture of you and my older brother Don found it. He showed my father and my sister Topaz that I had found you and assumed that you didn't want to come back to save your people…"

"What do you mean save *my* people?" Rose replied angrily and started to feel a sense of fear slip into her skin.

"I tried to stop the Draughtningrs from going after you, but they called me a lovesick fool and told me that I better tell them where I had last seen you or else." James was talking very quickly at this point, and Rose knew that she must be showing signs of lashing out. When he next spoke, Rose barely caught what he was saying. "So then I told them…"

"You told *them!*"

"…but I knew I had to try to get to you first, but when I found out where you were, they were already heading your way, so I called you." While he stopped to breathe, Rose realized she knew what was about to happen next.

"When the people after me entered my shop, I hung up on you. And you went to the place you said you would meet me, hoping that I would show up."

"When I saw you heading my way with the Draughtningrs right behind you, I knew I was too late and that the Draughtningrs were going to get you first. Then my brother, who must have followed me, wrestled me to the ground and told me that you would be dropped off at our place, where you would be told about the Tiara of Emerald Thorns." He stopped and look at her. "And how it would be your job to find it and that your people are relying on you."

"James, what do you mean by *my people relying on me*!" She said all of this with her eyes practically shooting sparks. She couldn't believe him. She was not the queen of a nation or, even more concerning, of an entire *planet*—she had secretly decided to believe that she was, perhaps, on a different one. She wanted the whole story, and James was going to tell her, whether he liked it or not. "I want the truth now, James!" she said, screaming at him once more.

"Fine, Rose," he said softly. "But would you please stop yelling and sit down?" he asked, "because it is a long story." She saw nothing wrong with the request and decided to sit on the bed.

"Well?" she said hotly, and he sat down and said,

"Rose, it would probably be best to start at the beginning." As he said this, Rose leaned back against her bed board, waiting for the tale to begin…

Heartington Castle

Igneous Stipes, who was bored out of his mind, sat on his throne while listening to his advisers on the goings-on in his kingdom of Aquamarine. They were sitting in Heartington Castle, which was at the center of the city, Decorus Regnum Corset. Igneous, who was tall and well built, pale, with fiery-orange eyes and charred-black hair, was thinking about things he would rather be doing and was getting annoyed. What did he care if the people wanted less taxes or that some of the women refused to be his servants for the required year? It really wasn't his problem. At that very moment, his trusted aide entered the room.

"All of you, clear out now, for I have told you many times, these petty problems do not concern me." His voice seemed so forceful and impressive; he liked it that way. While watching his advisers leave, he slowly approached the man who always got what he wanted done, no matter what it was. Closing the door as the last man left, he turned toward the newcomer, who was known as Exotius Obscurum.

Exotius Obscurum was built similar to his lord and master, but with some small differences. Exotius had a deep tan and had funny blue eyes that, in contrast with his hair, which was black with streaks of red and orange, made him recognizable by just about everyone. Which, thought the king, was a good thing, because if Exotius was entering the house of a subject, the subject knew that they were in trouble.

"So, Exotius, what real news is there for me to hear?" said the king as he approached him, gave him a quick glance, and then continued walking toward his throne. And in reaching it, he sat down. Now facing his servant, he waited for the answer.

"My King Igneous, I must inform you of the disappearance and reappearance of some members of two of the most revered families in our great kingdom." As he said this, the king looked at him, thinking about what he had said.

"Which two families are you speaking of, and who would dare leave a mark on their family name to venture out of this world without our permission?"

Exotius stared at him for a minute and then, as if choosing how to put something in the perfect order, spoke.

"My king, it was Liam and Aphra of the Draughtningr family and James of the Tungston family. They seemed to have wanted to beat the other family to something in that other world. I did not, however, see them reenter our world, but through my lines of communication, I am told that they have retuned."

Exotius waited for the king to reply. He did not have to wait long.

"You say the youngest Tungston boy left and returned, as he did about three years ago. I wonder what he has found in that world that is so interesting." Igneous looked at Exotius with a flame in his eye. "They don't call the king's flame revealing without reason do they Exotius? Now go find out what is so interesting in that other world."

"How would you like me to handle the situation? After all, it was only days ago that I convinced your new maid that saying no was a bad decision." Exotius smiled as he thought about that last statement.

"Whatever it takes, my friend," he said as he smiled evilly, "whatever it takes."

"Oh, by the way, there was said to be a young woman with black hair that was unconscious and being carried by the Draughtningrs." Exotius seemed to be saying this as an afterthought, but this afterthought worried the king.

"Did this woman have pale skin, a firm figure? Was she around twenty-one, and did she have green eyes?"

"Yes to the first three," he said, and just as the king let out a sigh of relief, he said, "her eyes weren't open." While Igneous was concerned, he decided not to show Exotius that side of him.

"I thought that you did not see them reenter our world?" he said as flames once again appeared behind his eyes. Lying was one thing that he would not tolerate. His aide seemed to realize what he had just said was contradictory to a previous statement.

"Sir," Exotius exclaimed with an air of apology in his tone, "it was the source that we discussed previously that told me about the girl."

The answer now fit the original story, but there was a lie in it somewhere; he could just feel it. He would have to just accept that he would not get a real answer, but he was going to ask again, and then there would be no false answers. He would be sure of that. Realizing that Exotius was still watching him, he made his face convincing enough so that he could turn and say that everything now seemed to fit.

"Go now," he said after convincing his aide that he did believe the story he had just been told, "find the troublemaker going by the name of James Tungston, and find out what is going on between these two distinguished families that, up until now, got on so well." He watched as Exotius turned to leave with a low bow. Alone once more, his mind fell on the strange young woman that was now on his planet. Shaking his head, he said quietly, "I'll think about the young woman later."

Thinking thoughtfully to himself once more, King Igneous watched Exotius exit the room to prepare to head to the house of Tungston to capture James and find out why Earth was so popular lately. The reason he loved what he did was because lies in his kingdom were punishable by law.

"Jenna!" he screamed, "Where is my horse, Infestus? Is he saddled and ready for me to ride?" A young woman of only nineteen years walked in, curtsied, and nodded solemnly and left without saying a word. He couldn't help but think that killing off her boyfriend had made such a huge improvement. Then, grabbing his cloak, he headed to the courtyard where he would mount Infestus and ride to the Draughtningr manor. What truly bothered him was that Devin Draughtningr would not do something as risky as to allow his children to further diminish his already-tainted trust with the king. "There is still a lot to be answered," he said softly to himself. As he began to approach his horse, he straightened his face. The questions would be answered, or there would be lives lost.

CHAPTER 3

The Truth about the Truth

The Courtyard of Heartington Castle

*E*xotius had, after being dismissed, let out a long, slow breath. He had almost blown his cover when he had answered the question about the black-haired woman. Yes, he thought, I was there. After all, when those three people had left, it was to him that the soldier who saw them leave had come. He told his men to guard the entrance to that other world, and when he did so, he also decided that he, too, would watch the entrance to Earth as well, but he would not be seen by any of his men. While remaining hidden, he watched as one by one his men left their posts, something he had, at the time, thought that he would make them regret doing. Yet it was as the last of his men had left that Don reentered the planet, and he had not been seen leaving. With him was his brother, James, who seemed less than pleased to be where he was.

"I told you not to go," Don said heatedly, "yet you did! You had your chance to do things the way that you wanted to, and you failed. You tried to hide your failure by not telling anyone what happened. You dishonored your family, and you forced us to turn against you for the time being, to go behind your back."

"She has a right to choose what she wants to do, to believe!" James retorted, "She deserves to live a life that she wishes, not the life that we want her to. You have no right to boss me around and, I did what I did for our cause. She wasn't ready to believe that she was from another world. You need to give these things tim—"

"No amount of time would have changed her mind!" Don said, cutting him off, "She didn't believe you. She was never going to believe you, and your love for her is only making you blind."

"I am not blinded by love!" shouted James, his cheeks turning a blotchy red.

"Yes, you are!" Don retorted, "The sooner you accept this, the sooner the fighting between us will stop. She is the key to freedom in this place, and you were throwing it out the door because you wanted to protect her."

"Well someone has to because you refuse to do so, which is why—" James was cut off once more.

"Which is why you didn't bring her back, why you wouldn't tell us where she was, why you still feel that you know best!" Don's face was outraged. "You are a fool, and it shames me to think that you, my own brother, would lie to stop us from finding her. We have little respect in the organization now, and I wasn't about to let you diminish it any further!"

James seemed to be lost for words. His anger was visible in his demeanor and in his breathing. He turned away from his brother and must have said something very quietly and insultingly, because Don Tungston's face was nothing short of shocked.

As the two brothers continued to move away from the entrance to Earth, Exotius was left to contemplate the very heated argument that he had just witnessed. There was something very odd going on. The brothers, as far as he knew, had always gotten on very well. Never had he heard of them fighting in such a brutal manner. There was more going on here than just two brothers arguing; there was something larger behind the arguing.

Exotius had very little time, however, to think on what had just happened, as there were now more people coming from that other planet. Aphra and Liam were reentering Aquamarine, but they were not alone. Liam was carrying a young woman with long black hair who appeared to be unconscious. Liam and Aphra, however, were not talking. In fact if he hadn't been looking right at the entrance, he probably wouldn't have seen them enter.

They seemed to want to get away from the entrance as fast as possible. This was the thing that troubled Exotius: this woman was not from that other world, for she had the markings of an Aquamarinian, not of an Earth creature. As they faded away into the night, his fears were heightened. He had long forgotten about the men that he had intended to punish. In fact he would use their absence to his advantage.

The thoughts of that evening had carried him all the way to the courtyard where his men awaited him. They were looking at him, expecting his orders. Yes, well, now that he remembered about punishing some of his men, he would do so when he reached Tungston Manor.

"Mount up!" he shouted, and as his men mounted their horses, he unsheathed his sword and looked at it. It needed to be sharpened, he thought. After placing it back in its sheath, he mounted his horse, Wildfire, and looking around at each of the men, he began to explain the plan.

"We have been ordered to go to Tungston Manor and take James Tungston into custody. He is of interest to the king and is to be unharmed." As he looked around at each of them, he could see that the message had been received.

"Move out."

He thought to himself that the truth about the truth was that no one wanted to hear it anyway.

CHAPTER 4

A Tiara of Emerald Thorns

Tungston Manor

"Many, many years ago, the battle for the crown of Aquamarine took place, and it started with one very ambitious yet very evil man named Igneous Stipes. Now Igneous, like every villain in a story you would read, possessed a quality that most people don't give into: doing whatever it takes to get what he wants. He wanted to rule. He wanted all the power, and he was going to get it no matter what. His first attempt was disastrous, having only a few men, and when they were caught, he was forced to flee."

"So he fled." Rose asked, "So what?"

"I'm getting there." James responded, "So anyway, he was forced to flee. When he was hiding, he was gathering loads of support from those that didn't like the present king. The king at that point in time was King Joseph Heartington…"

"Heartington?"

"Yes, Heartington," James replied, "may I continue?"

"Go ahead."

"And while many liked him, when he was younger, he had made many enemies. His wife, Joanna, had only produced one child, Nicholas Heartington, before dying of overexertion. King Joseph wanted to have a peaceful kingdom, but Igneous was set on creating chaos. He had found many who would willingly join his cause by now, and one of the last people to join was Exotius Obscurum, a man who was notorious for leaving a path of destruction and despair wherever he went. These two infamous men soon were well known across the planet, and wherever they went there was tragedy, and those who supported them were allowed to join and keep all that they owned. Those who didn't weren't as lucky."

"That's disgusting," Rose said with a look of revulsion, "you don't mean they were…"

"Killed," he said with a disturbed grin, "yeah, but it didn't stop there…

"The women were either sold as slaves or were paired up with men that Exotius liked a lot. These activities couldn't be ignored much longer. By the time King Joseph decided that he should probably intervene, the hand of chaos was already gripping the land.

"By this time his son, Nicholas, had found a wife by the name of Jemma, who was, while being fair, not the fairest ever seen with her well-built figure and her black hair, the likes of which could put the blackest of nights to shame. The king told his son to send his wife to a place of safety, for he would be joining his father on the field of battle."

"Did she flee?"

"Yes, for unbeknownst to her husband, she was pregnant with what turned out to be a boy who would later be named after his father.

"Anyway, the battle that took place between Igneous and King Joseph was gruesome, and while the king's men fought valiantly, when Igneous killed and decapitated the good king and his son, many of the men surrendered right there and then. Igneous declared himself king, and his best friend the leader of his army and security force. He seemed very confident that he had destroyed all the supporters of the old regime. There did come a day, however, that Nicholas Heartington II appeared. While the now very old Nicholas II seemed to not really know that he would have had Igneous's title, Exotius convinced the king that he was indeed a threat."

"Are you going to tell me that Igneous had him killed because his best friend thought him to be a threat?"

"Yeah," James replied, "but before he was executed, the king told, or ordered, I should say, Nicholas II to tell him where the family hid the famous jewel-producing roses. Nicholas looked at him and said that the roses will never produce anything for him. Nicholas was tortured for the information, and just before he died, he finally revealed the location of the roses. That night Nicholas's wife, Jane, fled their home with their adult son Neil and was never heard from again. And since Neil was never reported, the king never knew he existed. That evening Exotius was sent to bring the bushes inside the castle walls, and they were never heard of or seen again."

"Wow," Rose commented, "so where is the thing that involves me? I mean, there wasn't really anything about a Rose Heartington in that story. Yeah, there were *roses* and there were *Heartingtons*, but there wasn't a *Rose Heartington*."

"Rose, let me get there, OK?" James said, rather frustrated, "Well, while some folks seem to think that the story ended there, it didn't. That very evening a prophecy was made by an old woman by the name of Jasmine Traymeda, who was sworn to have lived for over two hundred years. In the prophecy it was said that the first girl to be born of a descendant of King Joseph would find the Tiara of Emerald Thorns that was produced by the emerald rose bush just before it was stolen. It is said that it will only reveal itself to that first daughter, and ever since, there has been a long search for her."

"James, I can see where you are going with this and—"

"Well there were seven sons that followed Nicholas Heartington I, and they ended with Nicholas V, for there was John, Stephen, and George in that line of boys. Nicholas V married Diane, and they had a little girl. This little girl was pale, like all of the Heartingtons, with green eyes that when she was calm, were like a calm ocean, but when upset were like electricity. The feature that surprised many, however, was her hair. For it was the same night-shaming black that Jemma Heartington had possessed. The proud parents decided that since she was meant to wear a tiara of thorns, there was no other name that would ever fit her but one. They named her Rose."

"Me?"

"Yes," James said, "you. Now understand that your birth was so celebrated that the king would have to be stupid not to notice that something was going on. He sent Exotius and another man, whom we know very little about, to find the source of celebration, and what Exotius found was the old woman, Jasmine Traymeda. She was a bystander in all of this, so she very freely told Exotius of the prophecy that was made many years previous. Exotius told the king, and Igneous told Exotius and the other man to find and kill you and your family."

"You're not serious."

"They went to your home, and while they found your mother and killed her, your father had already left for the planet of Earth with you in tow. Exotius and his counterpart were not fools, and they valued their lives as much as the next person. But it was Exotius who would have the most to lose if he failed. For you see, he was immortal, along with the king, but it did not mean that he couldn't be killed. He knew their immortality did not protect them from disease or fatal injury. Deciding that you probably would never be heard from again, he and the other man told the king that you and the rest of your family were dead and that he shouldn't worry."

"They lied?" Rose asked, shocked that he would risk his life on the fact that someone wouldn't find her. "Wasn't that risky?"

"Yeah," James replied, "but they didn't know about the secret organization of RTET: Rose and the Tiara of Emerald Thorns. My family has been part of it since it was started twenty-one years ago. It was the job of the members of this organization to relocate you when you were of age and return you to your home. It was also our job to aid you in any way possible and to help you realize who you were.

"As the years passed, we tried to figure out where the tiara might be hiding, where the best places to go first were. We also started a training organization that took ordinary people and made them into high-class warriors. We call ourselves the Thorns, and we stand for true justice and not what people have been forced to abide by and believe to be justice."

"So how can I even begin to help these people?" Rose asked, looking very worried now. "If you haven't noticed, I am accustomed to Earth traditions, and I have always been a follower. Where and when would I begin to search for the tiara, and how am I to defend myself?" she added, each word getting higher in pitch and coming out faster. She began to look around for answers. "I mean, you are trained to fight and protect, and here I am supposed to lead *you*. That would even sound ridiculous to a small child. James, what you have said, while making me feel honored, is completely freaking me out!"

"Rose, here is how it is going to work." James said in a soothing voice, "Before we go and look for the tiara, you will meet the members of both RTET and Thorns. We will fill you in on what we know and update you on the goings-on in the kingdom. Then we will discuss with you the ideas of where we might find the Tiara of Emerald Thorns."

"James, I think you're missing the point!" Rose said, now panicking, "I *can't defend myself!*"

"Rose," he whispered, "you think that we haven't figured on you being in this position?" Rose thought about that for a minute before uttering a no.

"Rose, you are going to be trained in the art of sword fighting." He said excitedly, "You will be taught the skills of archery, strife, and accuracy. Through Thorns you will learn how to act while thinking very quickly, how to be able to change your plans at second's notice and still have a good one. Finally, you will go into the Forest of Promise, and an animal will choose you as its equal. Once your equal has chosen you, a blade to match your very personality will be crafted by the best sword smith on the planet. Your armor will be made to match the color of your animal, and armor for your animal will bear a crest that is befitting for the both of you."

Rose thought about all of this for a moment. It was a lot to expect of someone who, up until a few hours ago, didn't know her whole story. She thought about what her mother might have been like and why, if she had done something so honorable, her father didn't tell her. It was as she was hearing this very thought in her mind that she decided there was only one thing left to do. "James, when do I start this mad affair?"

"We'll get ready to head to headquarters immediately," James replied excitedly, and he turned around and left the room.

Rose got up off of the bed, and after stretching she walked over to a painting that was so realistic, she could have reached into it and grabbed the tiara. There then came the shattering of glass from somewhere down the hallway. James and two other people, a young man and a young woman, came running into her room, locking the door behind themselves. James had a very hurt and sad look in his eyes. The other two, however, were getting a secret passageway open. Before she could question what was happening, and barely having time to grab the painting she was staring at, she was whisked into the cold and unwelcoming passageway. It was just before the door was closed that she saw a man looking through the window. He had charcoal-black hair with strips of red and orange alternating through it.

CHAPTER 5

Exotius's Discovery

Tungston Manor

It was foolish, and absolutely pointless, that someone would try to stop him from entering their house. Neil Tungston now lay dead on his own entranceway floor, with a blade mark right through his gut.

"Foolish old man." Exotius said with disgust etched through his voice as he looked at Neil. "Search the place. They have to be in here somewhere. Whoever you find, bring them to me immediately." He watched as his men scattered. As soon as he was alone, he began to head toward the end of the house that he knew held a room with many a famous painting. The men that he now had searching the house were the very men that had failed him a night ago. That was all part of the plan; they would be in the house while he conducted the last part of *his* plan.

As he walked past sculptures and suits of armor bearing the crests of many past Tungstons, he watched as the art motifs changed. There were many different types of paintings pertaining to and portraying one individual. There were twenty-one in all, and they showed the transformation of a little girl growing into a woman. The last three were much more detailed, as if the artist had a little more to go on than perhaps an idea. It was as he passed the last one that he noticed that she was dressed like a normal Aquamarinian, except for what was on her feet. She seemed to be wearing a pair of black boots more commonly found on the planet Earth. These pictures reminded him, unfortunately, of the woman he had seen a night ago.

"I wonder," Exotius said to himself as he took a final glance at the last painting before entering the room at the end of the hallway. "Ah, yes," he said aloud. This was indeed the room he had been looking for.

"What do we have here?" He walked over to a spot on the wall where there was a twelve-by-fourteen rectangular space of wall that was a different color from everywhere else. There had definitely been something here. It was as he was standing there that it struck him that this room was portraying the story of the Tiara of Emerald Thorns.

"The king will want to know about this, he said." And about how defiant Neil Tungston had been, refusing to tell him where his son went or to even let Exotius into the house, for that matter. It was as he was thinking about the king's response that he caught sight of the panoramic panting spanning the length of the room. As he walked toward it, his heart's pace began to quicken as he spotted what was at the end of the storytelling painting. There she was, the young woman in the hall, only she was twenty-one years younger when he had been sent to kill her; but he never got the chance to. There sat Rose.

"Well, that would explain why he wouldn't let me in, that treasonous, treacherous man." he said aloud. Then, he thought hotly, he would now have to explain this. This was also a problem, as he was sure that the young woman in the hall was the young woman that had entered the planet one night previous. I'd best take this with me, he thought, and with considerable ease he cut out the panoramic and rolled it up.

"Excuse me, sir," came a voice from behind him. He turned around slowly to face his best man holding out something rather strange. It was like a very small painting of the young woman in the hall, but it wasn't made of paint. "I found this in the bedroom of young James Tungston. It was hidden, being used as a bookmark." Exotius handed the rolled-up panoramic to the man and took the strange panting. He turned the strange painting over and saw the date: June 8, 1998. As Aquamarine kept a different calendar than Earth, it was hard to tell how old the thing was.

"Thank you," Exotius said with a touch of insignificance in his voice, "you may go and tell the others we discussed to leave the building. Tell them that a *message* is to be sent to the rest of the disloyal scum on this planet." As his soldier left the room, Exotius gave the small painting one last venomous look before putting it in his pocket and thinking up a story as to how the young woman had come to survive. He walked back down the hall and reentered the receiving hall. The old man lying dead on the floor never got to tell his side of the story. But what did he care? This man had been given a chance. Yet it was still a shame; the family was always well respected—that is, up until this point.

"Ah, well," Exotius sighed as he closed and barred the doors behind him, even though most of his men were still inside along with all of the *male* servants, for the king had no use for them. "Burn it down." The last part of the plan was to be followed without question. Some of the women started crying, and there were some looks of confusion about the order he was giving.

"Sir," said one of the men, "some of our men are still in there."

"Do as you're told before—"

"Sir, do you really thin—" Exotius grabbed hold of the man's neck after reopening the door, and he flung the man through it. The order, his order, was to be followed without question.

"If you had been smart, you wouldn't have questioned my authority," Exotius said with an evil glare in his eye. "But since you are not, you get to die along with the men you seem to have such a divine affection for." As he said this, he slammed the door, ordering the rest of the men who were not holding prisoners to bar the door.

"Now the rest of you, burn it down." As he said this, one of the women got loose, but only for a second. "And I'll take her with me."

As they mounted their horses, the smell of the burning building filled the air and the nostrils of everyone who was within a hundred meters of the spot. Exotius smiled at the young woman that was sitting behind him. She was crying silently and avoiding his gaze as he and his men picked up speed heading back toward the city of Decorus Regnum Corset and Heartington Castle, where he would give the king his update on the real problems in his kingdom and tell him of the mistake that was made twenty-one years ago.

It was as this thought passed through his mind that the skies finally unleashed their fury, showering them with rain, dazzling their eyes with lightning, and ramming their eardrums with thunder. The first sign, Exotius thought, that things were heading in a direction that King Igneous would obviously be displeased with.

As he reached the end of the drive, he decided to alter his course.

"There will be a change in plans," he said as the men looked up at him with looks of terror in their eyes, fearing that they would be thrown into the inferno as well. "We will be going to Draughtningr Manor to meet the king and to tell him of our discovery."

The looks of relief were everywhere, and as they continued in the newly ordered direction, Exotius smiled to himself. They all knew who had disobeyed his orders on that night, and only the disobedient ones were the ones who died that day. He loved being in control; what he didn't love was having to bring bad news to a king who was already in a mood that was less than good.

CHAPTER 6

Similar Circumstances

Draughtningr Manor

Draughtningr Manor was considered the most magnificent of all the manors on Aquamarine. The building itself was constructed out of granite that was inlaid with diamonds, in representation of the family stone. It was said to light up the heavens themselves when the sun hit the building just right, sparkling as though there was a chance that the sun would not return tomorrow.

It was to this historic building that Igneous Stipes was heading. The road that led to the manor was long and winding, with huge trees that seemed to be as old as the planet itself. These great trees were so large that it would take three grown men to hug the base of each of their trunks. As he rode down this lane of trees, he was beginning to notice things that were missing, like simple sounds of the gardener working, or maids gossiping as they went about their work. As he got to the end of the lane and entered the courtyard where the main entrance lay, he noticed that the once very lively manor now seemed deserted and still.

"Search the place," Igneous said as he dismounted his horse, "but do it quietly, just in case there are people hiding in there somewhere."

"You heard the king," said the captain in charge in his quietest voice, "get moving."

Igneous then entered through the main entryway. As he removed his riding gloves, he saw and knew right away that there was no chance that the Draughtningrs would be found here. The room was a disaster area, with papers scattered everywhere. People's belongings were among the mess, and yet there was one thing that was not to be found.

"Sir, there is no sign of human life in this building." Igneous turned to face the captain as he spoke. "I have also noticed that all the activity logs for the last twenty-one years are missing, along with all of their jewelry and family heirlooms, including the famous Crystal Lion of Jerard."

This was fishy, and it was as he was thinking about this that there was a great commotion outdoors. He left the great hall and the mess that lay inside of it, and he went outside just in time to see Exotius heading into the courtyard. He saw that on the back of almost every soldier's horse was a young woman. What had he done now? he thought angrily. He didn't need new maids.

"Exotius," he called out, "where in heaven's name did all of these women come from?" He knew that his voice alone would tell Exotius that he was not impressed. "I thought that I told you to go to Tungston Manor, not the maids convention!"

"We did go to Tungston Manor," said Exotius hotly. As if he felt his master was scolding him for a story that he had yet to explain. Then, after calming himself, he continued his report in a calmer tone. After telling the king of Neil Tungston's treachery and of the twenty-one paintings depicting the young woman with black hair. Then after telling him everything, he waited for the two things that he believed were sure to come: a scolding for letting the last Heartington live and a demand to see the strange, miniature painting.

"Exotius," Igneous spoke very quietly, sinisterly even, "why did that little girl that I sent you and my brother to kill, survive?" It was a simple question, he thought, yet he knew that it would have a complicated answer. "After all, you said that she was nothing more than a small child and therefore a small problem. Didn't you tell me, when you returned from that small house of Nicholas V and his wife, Diane, that they were all dead, that no one had been spared the steel of your blade? Yet here we are, almost twenty-one years later, and that little problem has become a mite larger one. Do you disagree?" Igneous could tell that Exotius was contemplating how to explain the situation that he was now in. It was an extraordinary feeling to have as much power over a single individual like he did.

"Your Majesty," Exotius said, his head bent in shame, "I have failed you. Twenty-one years ago, you sent me to the house of the last Heartingtons. I found only the wife of Nicholas V. Nicholas had fled to what I now believe to be Earth with their daughter. I killed only the mother that night. I am sorry to have failed you in such a pathetic way."

"Your excuse for lying to me has yet to be presented."

"Your Majesty," Exotius said in a sad and mournful tone, "it was the idea of your brother, Jonathan, to tell you that they were dead. I, on the other hand, wanted to tell you the truth and face the consequences, but your brother feared your wrath."

Well, thought the king, his brother would feel his wrath, a wrath that he had built over twenty-one years. His brother was going to have to answer to him, and his answer better be well thought out.

"Exotius, I would like to have that strange painting that you spoke of."

Exotius handed the photo to the king and then went back to his position. The king observed it and while doing so was thinking up a plan.

Turning to Exotius, he began to speak,

"You and your best men are to find and capture that girl and James Tungston. You are then to bring them to me. Do you think that you are able enough to do that?" The look that he got was not only reassuring; it was a humiliated look that told him he had made his point.

"Good." He exclaimed, "Then I will return to Heartington Castle, where I will be awaiting your report." Only after I have dealt with my brother's treachery, he thought. "After I return from the Stipes' summer home I will grant you an audience, after which I will start my research on the Tiara of Emerald Thorns."

Exotius sent half of his men with the king, with the women on their horses and them walking. The rest of his men were awaiting his orders.

"Search the place for clues as to where these people have disappeared to."

His orders were followed as soon as he had finished giving them. He turned to watch the king fade into the distance. He smiled, more to himself than to anyone else. The king would trust his word over his brother's, which was convenient because the story was true; there were just some minor differences. He had decided to lie about the family being dead, and his brother was afraid of his wrath, the wrath that would be presented if they were caught.

"Poor Jonathan."

CHAPTER 7

The Secret Passage

Somewhere under the city HawThorns

It was dark and cold in the tunnel of earth that the Draughtningrs were now traveling in. They had only had a few minutes' warning from their maid Marina, who came running from the end of the drive, explaining that the king himself was coming toward their home. With all possible haste, they made a grab for their weapons and most precious valuables and fled to the secret passage that had been there since the fight for the throne. Never had the family thought that they would need to use the now-ancient passageway again. Devin led his servants, along with his son and daughter, down the passage. They had sent a message to the other members RTET that they would be assembling in the Forest of Promise. Their hiding place was a clearing there and was well hidden. All this would be where they would plan their resistance and train Rose to fight and be the leader that she needed to become. This would have to be done quickly, as the king was already onto something.

"Father," Liam said from behind, "were we supposed to be waiting for the Tungstons at the intersection that we passed?"

Devin looked around at his son and the passage that he had just walked past. Sighing, he turned around and walked back toward the tunnel entrance, their servants groaning slightly under the weight of their loads. Marina Griffen, her mother, Pricilla, and her brother, Dathen, all were carrying items of great value, and a quick change in direction wasn't easy. They had the same animal, a Cocker Spaniel; however, all the animals were waiting for them in the forest already.

"They should have been here by now!" Aphra exclaimed, her face reflecting the fear that her father felt. The longer they all waited, the harder it became for them to stay still and calm.

"We can't stay here forever," sighed Devin. "They might not have made it. They might have been caught off guard, and they just might not have…" His words trailed off into space, as there were footsteps that could be heard from down the tunnel that they were gathered around.

"Hide quickly," Devin whispered. He had no idea who that could be, and he wasn't about to chance that the footsteps are the friendly sort. After all, they had been tricked once before, and that was how he and Neil had lost their wives. They would forever been haunted by their mistake.

"Where is Devin!" said a voice belonging to a man. "He said to meet him right here!"

"Don, calm down. They may just be running a little behind, so just calm—" The man's voice was cut off so quickly that part of his sentence clashed with that of a woman's.

"You know I think that panicking right now is completely justifiable, since we seem to either have gone the wrong way or the person who was supposed to have met you has been caught." The snap that was behind the words being spoken rang throughout the tunnel. There was then a long silence that followed, in which both groups seemed to be considering what they would do next. The group in the tunnel seemed to have made their decision, as they were now moving toward the Draughtningr party's hiding spots. As the strangers came into view, they were revealed to James, Don, Topaz, and a young woman that Devin assumed to be Rose.

"There isn't anyone here!" Rose said in a panic. "You said that those other people would be here to meet us and lead us to the new place of hiding." Her panic was reflected in the eyes of the other three. They all seemed lost as to what the next plan of action was.

Devin gave the signal signifying that it was safe to come out. As he stood up, relief spread over three of the four faces. Don walked right up to him and pulled out his sword.

"What was the code of which only the two of us would recognize? Answer me!" Don was staring right into Devin's eyes, his sword pressed against Devin's throat.

"A rosebud covers thorns like a cloak covers a sword." As soon as these words left Devin's mouth, Don's features eased, and his face showed relief.

"Sorry, but it was necessary after seeing that the tunnel had been empty the whole time that we had merged with it." His apology was genuine, and he seemed to be feeling a little guilt.

"I understand," Devin replied, "but now is not the time. The king was heading to our home, and I take it you met up with some of his men."

"Not just his men!" Don exclaimed with a look of revulsion. "Exotius came and paid us a visit with them. He killed our father and was after our brother James. I heard him talking to our dad before getting into the passage. He said that treason was punishable by death. I heard Father cry out and then silence. We barely got away." Don's story wasn't gripping by any stretch of the imagination; it was what was in it that was scary. Igneous was looking for those people who had gone to Earth to get the young woman in front of him.

"Do you think that he knows?" Devin's question hung in the air like a fog that was just thick enough to be visible. Everyone could feel it; it clung to the skin as though made of spider's silk and heightened fears. It was James that spoke first.

"I think that they may be curious to know why we left. I am sure that they are unaware that Rose is the daughter of Nicholas V." After this statement they fell into a deep silence once more. They all seemed to want to believe that the last part of James's statement was true, but the fact was that it was more likely than not that the king knew who Rose was.

"Well I hope you won't mind me being rude, but there are people after us, and I think that it would be a good idea to keep moving." Rose had broken through the silence with the sharpness and precision of a blade. Her eyes were moving from Don to Devin, waiting for the answer.

"Yes, she's right," Devin said, sort of off-balance, "if we stay here, we could very well get caught, and we do have a long way to go. The farther we get, the safer we are."

Rose was satisfied with his answer, and it showed in her eyes, for they had lost some of their electricity. As Devin and Don led the way out of the tunnel crossroads and into the tunnel that had been to their direct right, he wondered how the king would handle the situation that he was in. Never had the king ever dealt with disruption in his kingdom.

Devin looked at the woman who could certainly, with the right amount of training, lead a nation to freedom. But there was a lot that was still left to be done. They had to get everyone in the same place and still be hidden from the eyes of the king. The question still remained, however:

How did the king find out about Rose?

With this last question teasing his mind, he led them deeper into the underground system, with the last rays of light falling on the tunnel crossroads.

CHAPTER 8

Jonathan Stipes

Stipes' Summer Home

Constance was lying on an expensive sofa and sunning herself. Constance was Jonathan's great white leopard with red spots and was the animal that had chosen him many years ago in the Forest of Promise. While she was sunning herself with her amber eyes closed with pleasure, the heavy sound of footsteps alerted her that someone was entering the room. She opened her eyes and watched as Igneous Stipes, Jonathan's older brother and the king of Aquamarine, entered the room. He was looking about the room, obviously looking for his brother. It took him a few minutes to see Constance and give her a reproachful look.

"Where's Jonathan?" he asked with his voice revealing the anger that his face was successfully concealing.

"How frustrated you look, oh great and mighty king." Constance loved to taunt and pester him, especially when she had something that he wanted. She could tell that she was getting the best of him. Flames were dancing in his eyes. At this sign she smiled, revealing her white and pointy teeth.

"I'll ask again," he said, straining to keep his face straight, although he was starting to show his frustration. "Where's Jonathan?" His eyes were focused upon hers, and in seeing that she could, she decided to push him a bit further.

"But Your Majesty," she said, an evil grin replacing her humored one, "you are so smart that you should already know where to find him." The look that she received was venomous. She was loving every moment of it. However, she knew that she would have to tell him what he wanted or risk having something thrown at her. There was also a good chance that he would yell at her as well. The thing was, she couldn't help but continue to smile while he tried to calm himself to prepare for the next question that he was about to ask.

"Constance, where is my brother? And don't 'Your Majesty' me." His eyes looked as though flames were actually shooting out of them, and his mouth was twitching slightly.

I shouldn't, she thought, but I'm going to; it's just too hard to resist.

"But Your Majesty," she said, her smile widening with each word she spoke, "you're supposed to know all and see all."

At those very words, Igneous, with the swiftest of hand movements, sent a very expensive vase flying at her. Although he ended up missing, he had a look of great satisfaction on his face. One that said, "Don't push me next time."

Baring her teeth menacingly, she moved into the center of the room and glared at Igneous. She shouldn't have pushed him, and she knew that, but he's like a spoiled brat that gets everything that he wants.

"Where," he said between heaving breaths, "is Jonathan?" His eyes didn't leave hers. He continued to breathe heavily as he waited for her imminent answer. His eyes were losing their fire as he continued to breathe and she knew that he would most likely throw something else if she didn't answer him, and soon.

"Jonathan's rather attractive maid was granted a visit from him this afternoon. He told me to take messages, should there be someone that wanted to see him and should they wish to leave a message." At the end of her statement, she took a look at him, and deciding that now was as good a time as ever, she asked him,

"Would you like to leave a message?" Constance got the look commonly associated with more throwing.

"Go and get him." He said, "Now!"

His look is *very* convincing, she thought, but not really. But in deciding that it was better this way, she walked out of the room and started down the hallway. Why was she the messenger for the two of them all the time?

As Igneous waited, he thought about what he was going to say to his brother. He wanted to be terrifying and to make sure that his brother got the message that he was about to be sending. After all, he had been lied to for twenty-one years, and that was just unacceptable.

Constance was reentering the room and had a reproachful look upon her face. Her demeanor suggested that she was, in some way, in trouble.

"He will be in shortly and says that you could have waited at least an hour more." She watched as flames reentered the man's eyes.

"Also, he wants to know what was so urgent at nine o'clock in the evening. Jonathan feels that he is entitled to some enjoyment every now and then, just like you. That he had been planning this for a few days now." She looked back up and saw that he was getting ready to toss something at any moment.

"He also says that if this is because you are jealous, that you had her first and that you had your chance." She barely had time to jump out of the way as a second vase was sent in her direction.

"It wasn't me telling you that! It was your brother, and I would appreciate it if you would refrain from punishing me when I am the one that is relaying a message." Constance looked at Igneous, and after a few minutes of silence, he muttered a small apology that wasn't, as far as she could tell, heartfelt.

"If you don't mind," Constance added, breaking the silence, "I am going to go outside and leave you to fume and yell at someone other than me." At these words she turned toward the door and left without another word, her tail flicking gracefully from side to side.

"I thought that your animal was supposed to stand by your side!" he yelled after her, but she did not answer his taunt. He was left to wait alone in his brother's sitting room for about ten minutes and was considering going after him when Jonathan walked in.

Jonathan looked nothing like his older brother. He had pale skin, soft brown eyes, white-blond, wavy hair, and was well built. He was also handsome, which was a department that Igneous was lacking in. He was what his older brother called "a ladies' man," with most of the maids begging to work for him.

"Igneous!" he exclaimed, clearly wanting to sound shocked and surprised, "When did you get here?" The question was a dumb one, and it did nothing but annoy him.

"You know how long I have been here!" Igneous replied angrily, "Constance told you that I wished to see you, and *you* sent her back with some very cheeky responses."

Jonathan looked a little nervous now. Apparently he hadn't actually expected Constance to repeat his statements word for word.

"Igneous, let me explain," Jonathan pleaded, and in doing so breaking that dead silence that had fallen on them like a mist on a cool night, "I was enjoying myself and wasn't pleased about being interrupted. You know that I don't mean those things that I said, and I am sure that you would probably like an apology for my actions."

"You're right," Igneous exclaimed in a dangerously soft voice, "I do. Especially for the lie that I received twenty-one years ago." Igneous watched his brother's features for signs of weakness, but all he received was a look of total and utter confusion.

"What did I lie about twenty-one years ago?" Jonathan inquired with a quizzical expression on his face, "I never lie to you, as I am afraid to do so." Jonathan's confusion was no act; he clearly had forgotten his twenty-one year old treachery, along with the much-older prophecy. It's time that I reminded him, thought Igneous.

"Don't you remember the task I assigned you related to the prophecy of the Tiara of Emerald Thorns?" Igneous waited before continuing in a slow, soft, and deadly voice, "The girl named Rose, her parents, Diane and Nicholas Heartington V. How I told you to destroy the last of the Heartingtons. Is any of this aiding your memory, or has all of this been lost to the past?" Jonathan's face had been draining of its color steadily as Igneous spoke. Now that his older brother had finished, he looked as though he might be sick.

"You didn't think that I would find out, did you?" Igneous continued to watch his brother's reactions, and at this point his brother was turning a pale green in color. "If you did, you are sadly mistaken. It may have taken me twenty-one years, but I still found out. Yet you believed that you could get away with it and that they would never show up again."

"No! That wasn't what I was thinking at all!" shrieked Jonathan, whose voice was now high in pitch because he was no so panic-stricken, "It was Exotius's idea to lie and say that we had disposed of them. I wanted to tell you the truth!"

"Liar!" Igneous screamed in fury, with his fury etched in the creases of his face, "You convinced Exotius to lie! It was your idea! You didn't want to experience my anger at that particular point in time! Well, you are going to face it now!" At these words Jonathan cowered in fear at his brother's wrath.

"Now," Igneous said, his voice a forced calm, "Rose Heartington, who was once a little girl, is now a woman." Igneous's calm was fading. "She is now somewhere in this kingdom, on this planet!" Jonathan was paying very close attention to every word that escaped from his brother's mouth, with his eyes focused on Igneous himself.

"We have no idea where she is, and two of the most distinguished families have disappeared off the face of Aquamarine. They all need to be found, but more importantly that girl needs to be located." Igneous was looking at his brother, flames flickering in his eyes yet again.

"You and Exotius have one more chance to finish what you started. After that you will face my displeasure." Igneous glared at his brother. He wanted to make sure that Jonathan got the message that there would be no third chance. It was important that he did, or the whole point in coming to this place was wasted.

"What is it that you wish for me to do?" Jonathan asked. His voice resembled that of a man who was unsure that his head wasn't about to be cut off: being careful to say the right thing.

"Find the girl." Igneous said in a blunt and rather annoyed manner, "Find her before she has been chosen by an animal. If at all possible, before the resistance finds her. If they should find her, we won't be able to get within a mile of her existence. The resistance may be small, but they hide people like her so well." Igneous looked at his speechless and bombarded brother to see if he was going to argue with him.

"Then you are to bring her to me so that I may deal with her. Do you understand me?" Jonathan remained silent for a long time. Every few minutes or so, he would look at his brother. It remained like this for a while until Jonathan spoke.

"Igneous," Jonathan had spoken so suddenly that he had made Igneous jump slightly, "what if the small resistance, as you have deemed them, already has her in their care? What then, Your Majesty?"

"Then we will assemble our own army and intelligence unit. We will find the resistance, and we will find her." At these words Jonathan looked at his brother with an expression of eager anticipation.

"This time there will be no mistakes."

CHAPTER 9

The Passage behind the Bed Frame

Draughtningr Manor

*E*xotius was inside the manor of Devin Draughtningr. The trim, which connected the high walls of the main hall to the elaborately painted ceiling, was made out of gold leaf. The leaves were shaped into many intricate and decorative designs. This place was only second in grandeur and elegance to Heartington Castle.

Exotius thought, *Well, that was when it was spotless and everything was in its proper place.* This was not, however, the case at the moment. There were objects scattered everywhere. Closets were thrown open, their contents covering the surrounding area. Suits of armor knocked over, furniture upturned, the stairs littered with objects that had fallen from arms that had carried them in a hurry.

That's enough, he thought. This is no time to think on facts as to why the building looks terrible. He had a job to do, and that was not to analyze the grandeur of this magnificent building. He was here to find something, even though he didn't quite know what it was himself.

"Sir." Exotius turned around to find his new head man. He hadn't thought about the fact that he would need a new head man when he had locked all of the disobedient men in Tungston Manor and set fire to the place. But he liked his replacement.

"Sir, would you please explain what you would like us to look for?" There was something to be said for fear.

"Look for a secret door or something." Exotius said this in a dismissive sort of manner. Make it look as if you don't care, he thought.

41

"Sir, what if there is no such passage to be found?" Exotius stood there, thinking that "what if" wasn't acceptable. There was a doorway here somewhere, and should he go into a room after someone and find one, there would be serious consequences.

"You and your men will search this place from the largest room to the smallest cupboard, and should one inch of this place be overlooked, there will be severe consequences." That was good, but he needed something more; something that would scare them and eat at their minds to the point that they would be terrified of failing.

"You all have much more to lose than you realize, and should you fail, you will find out just how much you've got to lose." As he finished he looked around at the pale faces of his men. Their fear was on their faces, in their eyes, and their skin would have glowed like the moon if it had been night.

"Now," they all jumped as he spoke, "I hope that I have made myself clear." There were several soft-spoken "Yes, sirs," but the rest were still silent.

"Then get moving." They moved very quickly, all except one of them: a young man, eighteen, maybe. How I hate insubordinates, he thought.

"Is there something you don't understand, boy?" Exotius watched to see signs of weakness; there were, however, none.

"Is there something you wish to tell me?" Still there was no answer, but as he waited for one, he caught a glimpse of a small tattoo on the boy's lower left arm.

The tattoo was of a *T*, but it was pointy on all the ends, giving it the look of a dagger:

The boy was a Thorn, or even worse, a Cryptic Conspirator. Then he remembered that Cryptic Conspirators had a circle around theirs:

The boy seemed to be frozen to the spot where he was now standing.

"What's your name, boy?" Exotius demanded, and in doing so he listened to his voice ring in the large room as he awaited his answer.

"My name is Danny, sir," he said, adding as an afterthought, "Danny MacNeil."

The name was familiar, and then he remembered that one of the king's new maids had the last name MacNeil.

"Rachel MacNeil is your sister, is she not?" Bullseye. The boy suddenly became rigid, and his face hot.

"Yes, sir."

"Her animal is a white cat named Damien, is it not?"

"Yes, sir."

"Your animal is a serpent named Tormen, yes?"

"Yes, sir."

"That's what I thought. Now rumor has it that the mark on your left arm is that of the military resistance named the Thorns, because it is a *T*. Correct me if I'm mistaken, but if there is a ring around it, which yours does not have, it means that you are a Cryptic Conspirator." Exotius saw the rage in the eyes of the young man turn to fear, the fear of realization.

"I don't know what you're talking about." His shaky voice became high in pitch.

A lie if I ever saw one, Exotius thought.

"Your sister is rather good looking; one might even say she is pretty."

"So?"

"So, one wouldn't want anything bad to happen to her. It would be most *unfortunate*."

"You keep away from her!" The boy had finally snapped. His anger lined every word he spoke. He had even drawn his sword to defend himself.

"You won't win, Danny." Exotius said softly, and he snapped his fingers. In doing so flames controlled and even encircled the boy.

Suddenly a red snake shot out of the bedroom at the end of the long hallway to Exotius's right. It was bolting toward Exotius in an attempt to save its human. Exotius drew his sword calmly. The blade was the color of blood, and in four swift movements, he cut the snake into four equal pieces.

"Tormen!"

The snake would move no more. He was dead; nothing could change that.

Exotius moved his fingers in a strange but swift circular movement, and at once the flames surrounding Danny became ropes. The ropes tied first to his wrists and then tied his arms to his sides.

"Now," Exotius turned to the boy, smiling all the while, "let's be glad that the snake was not your sister, shall we?"

"Whatever you want, I'll never give to you! No information, nothing!" And he called Exotius a foul name just to prove that he was serious.

"Those are strong words, especially since they're coming from someone who has another's life or well-being on the line as well as their own." Exotius watched the boy glare at him for a while and then continued in a matter-of-fact tone, "Your sister is only safe as long as I want her to be. Should you not give me what it is I want, I will make her life most unpleasant. Am I clear?"

The boy was very quiet, unmoving, and his face, while harder to read than some, said to Exotius, "You win."

"How did the Draughtningrs escape this house without being seen?"

"I don't know."

"Oh, you don't, do you?" Exotius hit him hard, and when he still remained silent, Exotius took his drawn sword and slashed him across the chest. The cut wasn't life-threatening, but it was, for the individual possessing it, inconvenient.

"I will ask you this one last time, and be careful how you answer. How did the

Draughtningrs escape this manor without being seen?" The boy did not answer, but he looked toward the bedroom that Tormen had come from.

Exotius grabbed the boy by the scruff of the neck and pulled him down the long hallway to the bedroom. This room was very disorganized, even worse than the rest of the place, if possible. The one thing that was where it was supposed to be was the grand bed.

Exotius threw the boy to the floor and walked over to the bed. The frame was attached to the wall and was as tall as he was. It started on the floor and ended about three to four feet above the bed. Since he was taller than most, there was no reason that this wasn't the door that he had been looking for.

"How do you open the door, Danny?"

"Figure it out yourself, you murdering monster!"

Exotius, as much as he would like to, knew that he couldn't kill the boy— not yet, anyway. Then he spotted a painting which was hanging a little to one side. He walked over to it and turned it in the direction that it was tilting. The bed pushed forward, and the frame swung open.

Voices and feet were coming in his direction because of the noise caused by the passage being revealed. Exotius turned to the boy, raising his sword, and gave him some advice:

"You should have helped me, Danny. Now your sister will suffer because of you." Then he slashed at his chest a second time, sending a good three inches of his blade into him.

"Stupid boy." And with that he turned toward the passage behind the bed frame and marched into it with the rest of his men behind him.

CHAPTER 10

The House Made of Trees

The Edge of the Forest of Magus

*I*gneous was riding along the long, winding road, if it could be called that, which led to the edge of the Forest of Magus. The Forest of Magus eventually blended into the Forest of Promise. He had always thought of making them one forest, but something about the Forest of Magus always made him feel that they should have different names. The Forest of Magus was the home of what people called "the House Made of Trees," which was the home of Jasmine Traymeda. No one in the whole of Aquamarine knew how old the old woman was, but she was at least as old as Igneous himself.

"How much farther is her house?" Infestus had interrupted his thoughts. His horse, Infestus, was just like his master, and he was ominous, the color of gray ash and his voice, while being high in pitch, had a gruffness to it.

"We should be coming up on it soon now."

"Constance got the best of you again the day before last." He paused. "Why do you let her taunt you so?"

"She always has what I want for information. Therefore I have to let her taunt me in order to get my answer." It was a good response, but part of it was a lie, and Infestus knew it, but unlike Constance, he did not press the issue.

"This lane has nothing about it that I particularly like." Infestus murmured. "It is so spooky, and the ground feels as though the blood of the magical people who were killed here is still wet."

Igneous knew that the bloody history of the forest was always playing on the fears of the travelers that went through it. His horse was right in this case, however, because the ground sank slightly when one stepped down. This comment sent them into silence for the rest of their journey.

As they neared a small clearing, they noticed a change in the trees and the earth beneath their feet. The ground was hard and cold, as if it were forever frozen in winter; Infestus's hooves could not even dent it. The air felt as though there was a mist around them, though there was not a visible one. The trees were old, ancient, and twisted. If plants and trees could look evil, the ones that surrounded the home of Jasmine Traymeda certainly did. The most interesting part of the clearing was that the house in the middle of it was formed by the trees. Their trunks and branches had weaved together to form a house that had two small windows and a door made of branches that had locked together in just the right formation to allow them to open and close.

"This place gives me the willies," Infestus confessed to his master.

"Don't be ridiculous," Igneous said in order to ward off his own fears.

"Sorry, but I think that it is just unnatural that trees should grow in that form by themselves. I think that magic formed them, and you know how wary I am of cursed objects."

"It is not cursed!" Igneous thought for a minute and then asked, "And who told you that it was?" The anger in his voice was clearly there, and Infestus shuddered slightly at the tone.

"No one," he replied, "I just assumed that it was."

It was when Igneous was about to scorn Infestus further that Indifferens appeared seemingly out of nowhere and stood in front of Infestus's path. Infestus had barely enough time to stop, and in jolting nearly sent the king flying over his head.

"Sorry, Your Majesty."

"Be more careful."

Indifferens was the creature of and companion to Jasmine Traymeda. He was a cat that was of medium build, with colors of white, gold, and black. He stared at the king and Infestus with a stare that was second only to a dead man, with eyes of pale silver. He stared as though he was reading the minds of the two creatures in front of him. His eyes moved slowly from the eyes of Infestus to the eyes of the very agitated king. The king felt as though he was being pierced through the eyes by those of the cat.

"Indifferens, where is Jasmine Traymeda?" Igneous demanded.

"She is inside." Indifferens answered with a slow, low, and very raspy voice. "She has been expecting you, Igneous, and wishes to tell you that you are two days late."

Then with a slow swish of his tail, he stood up and began to walk slowly toward the House Made of Trees. When he was halfway there, he said in the same low and raspy voice, "Coming?"

Infestus gave Igneous a pleading look as he dismounted.

"Stay in the clearing, Infestus."

"Yes, Master."

With that Igneous followed and caught up with Indifferens in a few moments, but slowed to the cat's pace when he had and followed him inside the house made from trees as the door swung open, though no one had visibly opened it. Once Igneous was inside, the door closed. The clearing, which had been illuminated by the glow from the open door, now fell into darkness, in which silence enveloped everything.

Infestus, now alone, heard nothing, saw nothing, and the world around him was nothing. He hated being alone, but his master had told him to remain where he was. Then he heard something, or more like someone. No animal would make that much noise on purpose. Another loud crack of a twig, and he turned around just quick enough to see the outline of a man.

CHAPTER 11

Jasmine Traymeda's Indifference

The House Made of Trees

The room that Igneous had entered smelled of earth and moss. The room was filled with a dim, warm light, but its warmth only stretched so far, leaving a quarter of the room in cool shadows. There was a small fireplace directly across from the door, and on its mantle were all sorts of strange objects and glass jars. Some of the jars bore objects like eyes and fingers, while others held pickled puggles and the tongues of trasicores. It was enough to unsettle even the coldest of men. However, he was here on business and had no time to think on matters that were not connected to the task at hand.

Jasmine sat at a small table near the fire and held her back to him and was bent over something. He was just about to speak when she sat straight up and turned slowly to face him. She looked older than time and was very thin, with wispy hair and pale, gray-blue eyes that were almost like water. She wore tan-colored robes that went down to the floor. Her white hair was placed in a bun, with wispy strands of it out of place, seemingly floating in a nonexistent breeze. She walked slowly toward him, her eyes staring into his, and so intense was her gaze that he looked away.

"You have come to me," she said in a slow, throaty, and intense voice, "to learn what has become of the girl who is to inherit the thrown of Aquamarine that sits in the castle of Heartington, surrounded by the bejeweled garden and residing in the great city of Decorus Regnum Corset."

Here she paused, seeming to take in his reactions, and again those cold, pale, and almost calculating eyes seemed to be reading his innermost thoughts.

How did she know where he had hidden the rare bushes? Only a few men

51

were privy to this information and knew that he had made a second garden under the original in order to house the jewel-bearing bushes.

"Well," Jasmine sighed, "I would have thought you to have already known where she was, what she was up to, even in whose company she would be in. It appears that I was wrong, however; you're just as naive as you were when you thought you had completely finished the Heartington family the first time."

With these words she walked into a second room, through a doorway shaped out of an enormous root of the tree that made up the very house they were in. Her soft footsteps made a faint shuffling sound as she moved away from him.

Isn't that nice, Igneous thought sarcastically, she was able to point out everything that had gone wrong throughout the past two days, and now she has the gall to simply walk away from me! After all, he was the king of Aquamarine, and she was a subject under his domain. He deserved answers. Yes, in fact, she was obligated to tell him exactly what he wanted to know, when he wanted to know it, and how it was going to affect his life and livelihood.

"You're thinking too hard about things you ought not to, Mr. Stipes."

Indifferens had entered the room and was now sitting in an old wooden rocker. It had intricate twirls and whirls throughout and had scuffed the floor to the point that it had made a permanent dent in the rough wood floor. The chair slowly rocked back and forth, back and forth, as Indifferens groomed his forepaws; all the while his pale silver eyes were continuing to follow and read the king's every move.

"I don't know what you mean."

"Oh, but you do." Indifferens whispered as he carefully climbed out of the chair, which continued to rock as he approached the king. "You do. You want Traymeda to tell you where the girl is residing this very moment so that you may kill her, or perhaps turn her, for you have not yet made up your mind."

"I don't think my decisions are any of your business!" The king shouted in outrage. How dare this stupid animal speak of things that are far beyond its comprehension? But you know, he thought to himself, he's right; you haven't made up your mind yet. What are you going to do when you get ahold of her?

At that moment he was called back to his senses by the frantic whinnies of Infestus. He looked at Indifferens, whose gaze had left his being and was now focused on the door leading to the outside. Jasmine Traymeda had reentered the room.

"A stranger who brings news of the movements of your foe approaches the house of trees."

CHAPTER 12

The Traitor among Them

The king was ready for anything. After the last two days he had experienced, he knew that he would have no other choice but to be ready. But what if he had fallen into an ambush and Jasmine had just sent off a signal to the other side? Or…

But before his thought could be finished, Jasmine Traymeda had made her way to the door and was letting in a heavily cloaked figure that was surprisingly wet. Could it now be raining?

"You have traveled far and at great haste to reach a master that will be enraged by what you will say." Jasmine's words filled the room with mystery and anticipation.

It was as the stranger was about to speak that a purely silver Cocker Spaniel came into the room and was about to shake off the fur that was drenched in water when he noticed who was in the room. Upon noticing, he and the stranger performed a very low bow.

"Your Majesty, forgive us for intruding, but the news we have cannot wait." The voice belonged to a Dathen Griffen, a boy who had already established a place of usefulness when he joined the king's league of most secret informants.

Dathen was a tall, skinny boy of about eighteen, with light-brown hair and light-green eyes. He wasn't built for anything, really, except for work and hadn't been doing it very long, as he was more lanky than strong in looks. His silver Cocker Spaniel, Proditor, stood just inside the doorway. His fur was matted with rain water.

"I must tell you that the Draughtningrs and Tungstons are, at this very moment, making their way to the center of the Forest of Magus. Somewhere in this vast forest's center, they have a secret camp at which all of your greatest enemies are gathering to welcome the one they believe will lead the battle of victory against you. The one they believe is the rightful heir to the Tiara of Emerald Thorns."

Here he paused, as if he were some sort of great actor on a stage set specifically for him and his grand news. Those who were in the room were like his audience, and he was about to amaze them.

"This person would be no other than Rose Heartington, who I have learned survived our capture by living on a little-known planet called Earth, to which there was a secret door only known to the great kings of the past."

Igneous just stood there. He wasn't sure if he was impressed or furious. Maybe it was a little of both. After all, this stupid kid decided to leave the others to tell him this oh-so-important news. Yet he, in the process, left before he could learn of the secret camp that would have made his information so much more useful.

"It's Dathen, isn't it?" Igneous decided he would be charming at first; after all, this kid was loyal and willing to do whatever it was that his king asked. "I must say I'm impressed with all that you've learned."

"You are, Your Majesty?"

"Yes," Igneous mused, "I must also inform you, however, that you are not the first to come up with this information. In fact the only new information you have provided is simply that you could have served me a whole lot more effectively if you had remained with the Draughtningrs until you reached your destination."

It was at the end of this statement that Dathen shrank ever so slightly, and Proditor, had hidden behind him.

"Why, if I were in want of an information courier, I suspect I would have hired one, yet you took on the job without there being one to take." Igneous's voice had risen to a point of absolute destruction, and he was now only a foot or so from the cowering figures that were Dathen and Proditor.

"Sire," Dathen pleaded, "we thought that you should be told tha—"

"Did it look as though I were finished!"

"No, but—"

"Then why are you interrupting me!"

"Because—"

"Well!"

"Because we had thought that you had summoned us, sire."

These words had not come from the cowering figure of Dathen, but from Proditor, who had a proper-sounding sort of voice. It almost sounded like that of one's personal butler, whose nose might be lightly in the air. With his warm brown eyes still upon the king, he continued,

"It is clear that Your Majesty did not send the message, and we were tricked by someone in the RTET organization who may be a spy among us."

At these words Dathen, who at some point had ended up behind Proditor, was nodding in agreement, trying to convince Igneous that these were his feelings also.

"A king who rules with such fear should fear his own shadow, for who knows when it shall turn on him?" Jasmine had remained silent for most of the encounter between the two men and Proditor, but her voice had returned him to her house, the room with jars, and Indifferens's penetrating stare.

"For a loyalty held together by fear will latch itself onto whichever fear is greatest." Indifferens nodded in agreement as Jasmine spoke.

"Be warned that you seek something that may not be what you think it is." Jasmine looked him straight in the eyes as she continued in a tone-dead voice, "She who is meant to rule is not meant to lead and conquer in battle. She can unite but not fight, for fighting is against who she will become. She will wear the Tiara of Emerald Thorns but will not be the one to overthrow the king."

With these words Igneous, Dathen, and Proditor stared at her in confusion; this wasn't what the prophecy had spoken of.

"You told me that the Heartingtons' first female descendant would overthrow me." Rage was building in him now. "You told me that the Heartington line was the only one that stood in my way of being the true king."

"And it still is," she said calmly, "and she will."

"You make no sense!" he roared.

"You never listen to me," she spoke calmly, "or the meaning of what it is that I say."

"You speak in a twisted language," he fumed, "how could I possibly understand you!"

"If you were truly listening, you would understand all that I say and the meaning of all that I do." She said this with an air of impatience. "Now would you and your frightened servant please leave? I was in the middle of poaching some froakes eggs when you so rudely arrived two days late, Mr. Stipes."

With that she turned and went into the same room into which she had gone before and closed a very odd-shaped and heavy door.

"I will show you out, Mr. Stipes." And it was with those words that Indifferens led them to the door, waited for them to exit, and allowed the door to close without another word from the three of them.

"Your Majesty, I have been so worried. These strangers come from out of nowhere, and——" But Infestus was cut off by Igneous holding up his hand to silence him. He turned to Dathen.

"Get your horse. You are returning to Decorus Regnum Corset with me. I want to see how much you really know about the resistance that perhaps, under normal circumstances, you may not be able to tell me."

"Sir?"

"Oh, don't worry. You'll understand when we get there."

And with those words, his mind turned to the castle and the bejeweled garden that produced the Tiara of Emerald Thorns. This seemingly insignificant headdress was making his days turn from bad to worse. Not to mention he hated riding in the rain.

CHAPTER 13

The Organization RTET

In a System of Tunnels under the Forest of Magus

*R*ose was tired, her feet were killing her, and she was surrounded by people who didn't really know her at all. This war that they expected her to be at the forefront of just couldn't be because of her and her father. Her father, Nicholas, just couldn't be the man they were calling Nicholas Heartington V.

He was a tall man, her father, just over six feet, and despite his massive size was a very gentle and kind man. He had warm blue-hazel eyes and a full smile that seemed to brighten the dreariest of days. His hair had not been black like hers but a very dark brown, with just a slight bit of wave to it. He had never been one to allow violence as a means to an end.

Yet she thought as she continued down the tunnel, her father's explanations of why there was no family to visit or where her mother had gone had never been fully satisfactory. But why hadn't he told her all of this before...

"Ouch!"

She had just walked straight into James, who had stopped very suddenly, and almost dropped the painting she had been carrying. She hadn't realized how closely she had been following him.

"Shh," whispered Don, "there are voices up ahead."

"Do you suppose we've already been discovered?" Aphra inquired from behind Rose somewhere in the semidarkness.

At these words several swords were unsheathed, and they all held their breath.

"Who goes there!" The voice was male and deep. A brilliant light had appeared in the tunnel they were about to turn into.

"Show yourselves!" called another voice. This one was high and clearly female, yet it had a slight growl to it.

The light was growing brighter, and then suddenly moving figures appeared in the light, as if they had been born from it. Rose and the others raised their hands as a sort of shield to the light.

"I am Devin Draughtningr, and I have in my possession a basket of flowers in need of planting." There was silence after he finished speaking.

Then, as if in response to what Devin said, the light dimmed some, and Rose could finally see who had joined them.

The first speaker was a man of medium height, maybe five ten, but his massive build and hard frame seemed to make up for his lack of height. He had razor-sharp blue eyes, almost like those of a bird of prey. Then there was his hair, sharply cut, sandy blond that probably would be wavy if it was allowed to grow out some. His attire was quite something, too, dressed in armor from head to toe, and it was almost all black, except for some streaks of silver throughout, and on the chest plate, a single rose was engraved.

"Devin," he said in a sort of grunt, "you could have given me some warning. After all, it's not like you to do things so spur-of-the-moment."

"You could have been killed in one of your own ingenious tunnels."

Rose looked all over for the speaker and then realized, in almost complete shock, that it had come from the black tiger right behind her.

The tiger looked right into Rose's green eyes, scanning what must have been her innermost soul with his gray eyes.

A distorted, birdlike noise came from somewhere on her left, and there she saw a great, all-gray hippogriff: all gray except for the tips of its wings, which were white. It had fixed its gold eyes on the group and then spoke.

"I agree with Evan and Allegiance," it said in a high, shrieky voice. "Why weren't we informed that you intended to move the girl?"

Excuse me, thought Rose, but I have a name, and if animals are unable to use it, then I think I'll just be leaving now, thank you. Deciding that she would rather not look at the two animals, she turned her attention to the new woman in the room. Her light, strawberry-blond hair was loosely braided with wisps that had freed themselves from the general bunch. She had soft brown eyes that just echoed warmth to Rose. She was about the same height as Rose. Actually,

Rose thought, she could be taller. She seemed to be the same sort of build as Evan and was wearing the same armor, except where his was accented with silver, hers was gray.

"Nightmare, Allegiance, where are your manners!?" Her high voice rang through the cave once more. "There is, I'm sure, a good explanation, but now is not the time, and here not the place."

"Vengeance is right." Evan looked around as if the walls had eyes and ears. "We must get back to camp and figure this all out there."

Hopefully we are almost there, thought Rose.

"Dathen?" Marina said in a shocked sort of way "Dathen?!"

Everyone looked around as if he were about to pop out of thin air. Then most everyone looked very grim.

"How long has he been missing, I wonder?" Devin said in a quizzical sort of voice.

"He could have slipped away at any time, and we wouldn't have noticed until we stopped to see if everyone was all right," hissed James with fire in his eyes. "Who knows when he left and how much he really knows."

"I always thought he was a little too inquisitive," pondered Aphra. "He really didn't need to know so much, as he was only a servant, but I thought nothing of it."

Oh great, thought Rose, now we have a spy on our hands. Wait, she thought, what's wrong with me—*we, our.* I'm not part of all of this—or am I? No, stop kidding yourself, this isn't about you, remember…or is it?

"Wait, what are you all saying?" Pricilla squeaked with horror and fear, her gray, curly hair falling out of its knot, her pale green eyes filling with tears. "Are you saying Dathen is a spy for the king? That he has been informing on all of us?"

Rose thought that must be so awful to comprehend, and she felt bad for that frail-looking woman.

"Mother," Marina spoke softly, her warm, hazel-green eyes staring into her mother's, "This is not your fault. You raised him the only way you knew how after Father died." Marina's black, curly hair shook as she did with anger at her brother, her thin frame as strong in will as she was physically.

"I'm sorry, ladies, but now is not the time." While Liam spoke these words, Don and Topaz were nodding in agreement.

"Especially in light of these new facts, I suggest that we move on from this place, and once we reach our destination, discuss this and all previous matters in full."

And with Don's final two words, everyone was gathering their things—everyone but Pricilla, who seemed unable to find the strength to lift her load. As her daughter was about to try to manage it, Rose held out her hand.

"Let me share your load."

Pricilla looked stunned, and everyone stopped.

"I don't have anything to carry except my feet, so I thought I might be able to help you."

No one spoke, but they continued to stare just fine. Then James walked over to where the three women were standing and held out his hands too.

"I think I might be able to spare a hand as well."

With that James carried his own load plus some of Pricilla's. Rose too carried a small load of objects, leaving Pricilla to carry only her grief. Now, Rose thought, I have more to concentrate on besides my thoughts. Oh, how much longer to we have to go before we're there? Oh, Rose, she thought, stop complaining.

"Wait."

Rose jumped slightly and dropped a few things in the process.

Nightmare was looking at all of them with incredibly focused eyes. Her head then turned to the tunnel. "I think we should make sure that we can't be followed from this point on."

Allegiance turned to look at Evan and then the others. "It could mean we leave the fate of others like us up to the king." His eyes were looking to see if anyone objected.

"Evan," Aphra whispered, "are there any more of us to come?"

"The Cryptic Conspirators have already joined us, and all the Thorns have been in camp for weeks." Evan pondered for a few more seconds. "Vengeance, is there anyone else I should be expecting?"

"No."Vengeance sighed, "Danny was killed, my sources tell me, and his sister has decided to stay in position in case we need her. She has also sent information my way that some of the others are remaining to help from the inside."

"So," said Liam.

"So," stated Don.

There was silence. It was almost like they were at a funeral and were about to bury any hope of going back to their lives the way they were before. Aphra, James, and Topaz exchanged glances and then took several steps to where Nightmare and Allegiance were standing. They looked back at the others and then tied several ropes to the beams holding up the walls and ceiling. They walked as far back as they could go and looked at the others.

"Get ready to run, everyone!" cried James.

Then he, Topaz, Aphra, and the two animals pulled hard, and everyone bolted down the passageway. They heard the loud rumbling of the walls caving in behind them, and Rose feared the worst for those that had done the pulling.

Soon they all stopped, out of breath and exhausted.

"James?!" Rose called, starting to panic as she saw everyone but him in the area. "*James!*"

"Stop your hollering, Rose," James emerged from the cloud of dust and was covered in the stuff. "I'm fine."

Then without thinking she dropped everything she was holding and belted him in the jaw. Now her hand hurt, but so did her heart; she had feared that she had lost him and knew that she still loved him.

"You are the weirdest woman," he said, standing up, shaking his head, and smiling, "that I have ever known."

"And you are the biggest ass I have ever met."

Then she ran forward, and they hugged each other.

"Are all women raised that way on Earth?" Aphra questioned Don.

"Heaven help the men if they are," Don said, petrified and puzzled.

"We still have a little ways yet, ladies and gentlemen," came Evan's voice from up ahead.

Rose walked with James the rest of the way, carrying her share and the painting. She listened as James told her all about how the tunnels were built and how it had been a huge accomplishment to complete them without the king finding out. He told her all about his horse, Valor, and about the time when he had first met him.

"I wandered for two days in the Forest of Promise before I came upon him. Valor was great in size and domineer. He was black with fine streaks of emerald throughout and happened to be drinking from a pool when I saw him. His eyes were the color of tourmaline, and he looked up from the water and stared right into my eyes with his pale watery ones.

"'James Tungston,' he said in a hard, crisp voice, 'Do you feel worthy of being my rider and my companion through the course of our lives?'

"I remember thinking to myself that there was no way that I could be worthy of him and all of his magnificence."

"What did you say, then?" Rose asked as they continued to walk.

"I said, 'No, I don't think that I am.'"

"Then he strode over to me and said, 'I think, then, that you and I will get along fine.'"

"After that he said that I could mount him, and we rode back to camp, where they outfitted me in black and green armor and created my sword, which I called Truth."

"That sounds incredible," Rose sighed, "it's like he knew what you would say and already decided that you were a good match for him."

"He did."

"I don't think any animal would want to make a journey with me through my life," Rose said in a dull voice. "Why would they? After all, I wasn't even raised here and wouldn't deserve any that would choose me."

"Don't be so hard on yourself," James said with a small smile. "You might be surprised by what you're capable of. I mean——"

But here he was cut off, as they had begun to walk upward, and then suddenly they were enveloped in brilliant sunlight.

"Welcome, Rose Heartington," said Evan, "to the camp of Rose and the Tiara of Emerald Thorns.

CHAPTER 14

Defining Constance

On the Road to Decorus Regnum Corset

*J*onathan Stipes was exhausted; never had he been so tired. Well, that wasn't completely true, there was one other time, twenty-one years previous, when he had been this tired, maybe even more so. The path he was on was rocky and uneven, full of knolls and tree roots sticking up to trip those who weren't paying attention. This path was through a mostly wooded area, and that was due to the fact that the road to the Stipes' summer home had been carved out of the Mendacious Forest. The path had been created some two hundred years previous, and the parts that had been cut away had long since grown back in.

"You're being too quiet, Jonathan," Constance's voice seemed to come from far away. "I hope that you are not still angry with me for taunting your brother."

"No," he sighed, "I'm just thinking about the situation that we are now in. Or maybe I should rephrase and say 'mess.'"

"What kind of mess?" Constance questioned, although she only halfheartedly asked it; she had begun to chase a small sort of creature off the road.

Whatever the creature was, it didn't strike Jonathan as important; not now, anyway. That matter was a mere trifle compared to what his brother might do to him. Igneous had been furious with him and said that he had lied: not only that he lied, but that the idea to lie had been Jonathan's idea and not Exotius's.

"Where would he have gotten that idea?" he asked out loud.

"Where would who get what idea?" Constance inquired again, only sounding passively interested. Her full attention was now directed on the road she was walking on and trying not to get herself too much dirtier.

"Igneous," Jonathan hissed, "he thought that it had been my idea to lie about the girl and her father twenty-one years ago."

63

"It wasn't?" she said absentmindedly but moved away ever so slightly at his angered gaze.

He was already frustrated, and now she was adding to it. In many ways the horse he was riding, which was normal, was more loyal and interested than his animal. This, he thought, was quite funny, considering her name was supposed to imply that those very qualities existed in her.

Constance had, like all the animals paired with an Aquamarinian, come from the Forest of Promise. She had been the one to choose him, and they then and there became what was called companions for life. He couldn't remember how long it was until she found him or why she had decided to choose him, but she had, and now he was stuck with her. There were times that she wasn't so bad, but then there were moments that he wished he could take her back. After all, it had been more than a century since she had happened upon him, and he felt that they were far different than they were then.

"You are thinking hard again." Her voice seemed to come from a completely different and distant land.

"You want to know how I can tell?" Here she paused for effect. "I can tell because your face is doing that funny thing where your eyebrows furrow, your nose scrunches up, and your mouth begins to twitch ever so slightly."

At these words he was drawn back to reality and found her staring up at him, slightly agitated at being ignored, as he seemed to miss some of the previous statement.

"What!?" Jonathan hissed at her. He was aggravated himself now, due to the fact that she seemed to think it was all about her.

"Well," she said, doing her best imitation of innocence, "due to the fact that I have paws with claws and not fingers with nails, I cannot open the doors before us leading into the city. Nor, for that matter, could I turn the key to unlock them."

"What?" Jonathan exclaimed aloud.

I don't believe it, he thought, we're here already? Now he had to make a choice. He could go into the city and then into the Castle of Heartington; there he could wait for his brother to return. Or, he thought, I could join Exotius on his hunt for the girl.

"Hello!" Constance purred, but a soft growl lurked in the depths of that purr.

Ignore her, he thought, I need to figure this out. If I wait for Igneous, he will be livid that I stood by and did nothing. However, he told himself, you and Exotius do not get along very well. It was a fact that the two of them had actually never got along, due to how Exotius conducted himself.

"Jonathan!" There was no pretend purr this time, and as he looked down at her, he saw that she was now pacing, her movements filled with aggravation and disgust. Her amber eyes piercing his very existence.

Shut up! his mind shouted this angrily. After thinking about it, he had decided that there was no true bright side in either situation, and he would need to pick the lesser of the evils: his brother's fury or Exotius's dislike.

"Igneous is scarier," he voiced aloud to the gate more than anyone else and began to take the path around the city, leaving a very confused and disgusted Constance right where she was standing.

"Wait," she growled angrily, catching up in the process, "are you telling me we aren't going to the castle?"

"Nope."

"Then why did you have me stand there forever just to abruptly turn the other way and start around the city?"

"I thought," he said through clenched teeth, "that your name meant you were going to stick with me and the decisions I make."

"Constance can have several meanings," she muttered curtly, "and it isn't like I abandoned you at any point in time. I am still with you."

"But are you *with* me?" he mused.

"I don't know what you mean by that," she growled shortly.

This heated discussion sent them into a silence as they continued around the city walls toward the road located at the entrance on the other side. Their path was hilly, and the silence strained. Each wished to speak to the other but wasn't sure about what to say and didn't want to be the first to apologize to the other.

Then Jonathan heard an "Ouch!" followed by a low growl and wince. He turned to see that Constance had stubbed her left rear paw and was now limping.

"That sounded painful."

"It was," she growled.

"That's karma for you." He grinned.

"Karma for what!" She limped on, continuing to glare at him.

"Karma for pissing Igneous off."

"Oh, I keep this world in balance when I get under his skin." She smiled. "Besides, you have to admit you enjoy me making him miserable."

"Why would I enjoy you taunting him?" Jonathan exclaimed. "Whenever you taunt him, it comes back to haunt me."

"Admit it: you love seeing him miserable." Her toothy grin was sharp and annoying. "Not only because he makes you miserable but because he is so high up there on his mountain of greatness that it is fun to watch him fall off and flat on his face."

It was true; Jonathan did gain some satisfaction from Constance's ability to get under his brother's dragon hide, or skin, as she called it.

At this point the hills were becoming level, and the road was becoming wider. They had reached the front gate.

Decorus Regnum Corset was the largest city on Aquamarine. While it was grand, it seemed less so when compared to the Mountains of Treachery just to the north and east. It did seem far more solid in comparison to the River Luminis that flowed through the city and which they had already crossed.

"Well, have you made up your mind yet?" Constance had a patience level that rivaled his brother's.

"Made up my mind about what?" He pretended that he didn't know what it was that she was insinuating.

Rolling her eyes and staring at the sky, seeming to ask why, she reiterated her question with more clarity: "Are you going to the castle, or are you going to look for Exoti—"

But she had stopped and was looking in the direction of the road that led to the city of Haw Thorns.

"Now that's nice," he said. "You start to ask a question and don't even finish…" But his sentence was lost because of what he saw coming toward them.

It was Exotius and a quarter of the band of soldiers he had left with. They looked as though they had been rolling around in the dirt.

As they approached, Constance turned to Exotius and taunted, "Your immortality is sure to be in jeopardy now."

"Since things didn't end the way I wanted them to," he glowered at her with those awful eyes, "Jonathan's immortality is in danger too."

"Excuse me!" Jonathan would not be threatened in such a manner. "I think you forget that I am the king's brother!"

"Oh no, I didn't." Exotius said through gritted teeth, "In fact I quite enjoyed telling *your* brother that you're the one who wanted to lie to him."

"I noticed."

"Well, it's good to know you noticed something."

"Must be nice to feel so full of one's self."

"Why, you stupid—"

But the rest of Exotius's statement was lost, as Constance had let out a growl and roar that sent the horses into a tizzy. So much so that they were practically throwing their riders off in fear.

"Constance," Exotius screamed over the ruckus, "you are a huge pain in the—" But he didn't finish his statement for a second time as he fell to the ground. Standing up and pulling himself together, he grabbed his horse, Wildfire's reigns and calmed him. The rest of his men attempted to do the same, although some were still shaking a little after it was all over.

"Why aren't you back with the girl!?" Jonathan said coldly. "Igneous will be livid that you didn't get her."

"Well it couldn't be helped," Exotius grumbled. "We were hot on her trail when the worst possible thing happened…"

CHAPTER 15

The Dead End

A Few Days Previous at Draughtningr Manor

" ... Stupid boy," Exotius said as he stepped over his body and led his men through the entrance and began their trek through the passageway.

These tunnels were old, and so were the markings for them; such markings hadn't been used since the Great Battle for Aquamarine.

"Good thing I was around then," he said aloud. His men were exchanging puzzled, fearful looks. They all thought he was losing it, but no man would dare say so.

"These markings will lead us toward our foe as easily as if he were our guide—or should I say 'she'?" Exotius exclaimed, almost laughing at the stupidity of it all. Here there was a secret tunnel, or maybe even a series of tunnels, with clear, discernible markings telling him, their foe, where to go.

He then led his men down the left tunnel and walked a ways. Here and there things had been dropped, valuable things, things that would normally be missed. Yet they had been left behind in haste so as to flee from him and their king. The walk began to feel long, and while he could go on forever, his men would soon be—what was that Earth phrase?—dropping like flies.

"We'll rest here for a while," Exotius said. He liked the power he heard in his voice.

Sighing was heard from every direction except in front of him, and one by one the men began to sit down, and some various forms of snoring followed.

"Humans." He shook his head and began to walk a little farther on.

As he turned the bend, he found himself in what would be almost like a town square aboveground. There were tunnels coming from every direction.

Some tunnels were labeled. Others were not, but one label caught his eye: 'Tungston Manor'.

"So," he said aloud, thinking all the while, "James, Topaz, Don, and the woman had all escaped in the same manner as the Draughtningr family."

That must have been a long walk, especially with an Earth-raised woman in tow. I bet, he thought, grinning to himself, that she probably complained the whole way here, and she most likely moaned when they said they had to keep going.

His mind then turned to the other symbols. Some referred to the names of prominent families. Yet others referred to towns and a few cities. There was one symbol that he knew was going to lead him to that treacherous, treasonous band of rebels. The *T* on that foolish boy's arm would ultimately mark the path to the girl. The reason being that one tunnel had that very symbol, as large as life, above it.

"Fools," he hissed satisfactorily. After taking one more good look around, he made his way back down the tunnel he came from. Once he reached his men, he then sat down and waited for them to recuperate.

After only a few hours' rest, he made all of them get up. As he took a quick look around, he noticed that some of the men looked as though they might groan. However, as he caught their eye, they seemed to think better of doing so.

"We *will* make better time than these villainous traitors," he said with a sureness he was certain that some of them wished they had, "for they have women and valuables that they must bring with them."

But it was not only possessions and people that he hoped would slow his enemy down, but a spy that had been carefully placed within their midst. His hope was that this spy would remain undiscovered and learn as much as possible about the operations of his foe.

He led them down tunnel after tunnel, a left, a right, two more lefts, and then straight on. It will be a thrill, he thought venomously, to catch them after he had to go through all this trouble to find and capture them. Not only the girl and the two families, but the rest of that puny, worthless organization known only as RTET that had been a thorn in his and the king's sides for a very long time.

It was as he was thinking about what he was going to do when he got his hands on them that something caught his eye, and he stopped. The great Crystal

Lion of Jerard sat there before him, poised as if to pounce on the first passerby. It could be a trap, he thought, or it could have become too heavy for them. Heavy or not, the Draughtningrs wouldn't want to leave this lion if they had the choice.

"You two retrieve that lion." Exotius watched as his two men walked forward to lift it.

Suddenly the center of the crystal lion glowed, and with only a second's warning, Exotius screamed, "Take cover!" And with those words, the lion exploded, sending shards of crystal in every direction. He had only enough time to take cover in the next tunnel.

"Well!?" he shouted in question and disgust.

"Creg, Alick, and Alistair are dead. Sean and Maude are injured."

"I have no time to deal with injured men," Exotius said with an air of impatience. "Take care of the problem, Draco, and the rest of you, move out."

Draco was the new head of the men he was leading, and he had decided to learn his name since he seemed to follow orders well enough. After all, it wasn't his fault that those men did not get out of the way in time. I mean, he thought, it wasn't like I asked them to do something impossible. I got out of the way without a problem.

There were cries of pain, then there was silence, and his remaining men continued down the next passageway behind him. This one had a lower ceiling and was narrower as well. Not only had it changed in size but in temperature too; it was cooler, and there was more moisture in the air they were breathing.

"Strange," he said to himself and thinking aloud, "the tunnels have changed as if the environment above had done so."

He began to notice tree roots here and there along the tunnel walls. The roots had tiny beads of water resting on them and were moving very slowly, as if the laws of gravity and matter ceased to exist. Despite the evident moisture, the ground under their feet remained hard, and as they continued down the tunnel, it became steadily darker. Not only was it darker, but the other tunnels began to converge on this one until there were no more branches merging with it. As they continued, darkness seemed to swallow them. Just when he was about to order his men to light some torches, the cave was filled with a cool blue light.

The beads of water had become little beads of light that, while emitting enough light to see where they were going, weren't bright enough for seeing much else.

"Sir?"

It was Draco, and Exotius knew what the question would be.

"We will stop for a while." I suppose, he thought, if these foolish Aquamarinains really need it.

As was custom to such an announcement, sighs of relief and some various forms of snoring followed, disturbing an otherwise empty and silent tunnel. As he was sitting, a single bead of water caught his eye. It was one of the more brilliant ones, and as he watched, its brilliant light was extinguished as the root absorbed it.

I must be under the Forest of Magus, he thought, for nothing else could explain the strange occurrences in this tunnel.

Then there were voices. As he heard them, he noted that their voices seemed muffled, making them seem very distant. He started to move toward the tunnel entrance when he heard a crunching noise that merged into a rumble. It was low, then it was louder, and then louder than that.

"Get up, all of you!" he ordered, practically yelling himself hoarse over the noise of the collapsing tunnel.

"Don't just stand there—move!" As he said these words, one fell behind them, and with a cry for help, he was silenced by the thunderous roar of earth and trees.

Exotius only stopped when the thunder stopped and turned to see that they had run quite a distance back in the direction he started in. He could tell because it was lighter, and the beads were gone. He had only a few men left. Then there was the irreversible knowledge that he would have to return and tell the king that a *cave-in*, of all things, had stopped him in his tracks.

In reading the sign closest to him, he saw it led to a building in HawThorns.

"This way."

It took almost a day to get aboveground in HawThorns and for the animals to readjust to the light. Exotius hadn't allowed the animals to stay behind and become a sitting target for an enemy, yet the animals seemed to be suffering because of his decision. His men and their animals were wrecks and were now complaining. Why, he didn't know; they were still alive. Draco had died in the collapsing cave, and Yaven was his new head.

"They look unfit to be led by you," Wildfire whinnied. His black mane rippled in the wind, his bloodred form stood tall, and his ash eyes stared at Exotius.

"I don't get to choose who follows me—completely," he sighed.

"Where to now, master?"

"Back to the castle," he said with reproach. "And hope that the king hears our story before he passes judgment."

At these words he and his men began their day-long trek to the city of Decorus Regnum Corset, and hopefully the king wouldn't be there waiting for them. It was as they approached the city's spectacular gate that two figures reached the front of the city as well.

Constance was clearly visible from a distance, due to her white body and red spots, and therefore it must be Jonathan on the horse beside her...

"That's your story, then," Constance mused, "I would have thought there would have been more killing in it."

"Shut up, Constance," Jonathan groaned.

"That's enough," Exotius growled as Constance was about to make a retort. "We haven't time for this petty, pointless bickering."

"Yes, Constance, why don't you try to keep that toothy trap of yours shut?" Wildfire said in a sharp, high voice.

Exotius was tired of all the stupidity in this world and wondered if the planet Earth was different.

"Let us go to the castle," he said firmly and looking straight at Jonathan. "There we can make a plan of action and lay out our explanation for the king."

"How," said an exasperated Jonathan, "are we to explain this?"

And with that they entered the city and prepared for their destined fate.

CHAPTER 16

The Task at Hand

In the Bejeweled Garden

Igneous sat on a rock in the center of the bejeweled garden and was staring at the rose bush that had, at one time, produced emeralds for the true ruler of Aquamarine. The bush was said to produce flowers of emerald green, and at moments the blooms would be made of solid emeralds, each petal more brilliant than the other.

It was this particular bush that was thought to have produced the famed *Tiara of Emerald Thorns*. No one knew what it looked like or if the legend was really true; no one except him. He had seen it only once, when the bush had been growing it; though at the time he had thought nothing of it.

The tiara was simple and elegant, set in a white-gold frame with emerald thorns on the frame. But when it had been finished, it disappeared off of the stem, magicked to some hidden location. He knew that by having a general idea of how it looked, he had the advantage of finding it, but where to look had always been another story.

"It could be anywhere," he said aloud, almost hoping the plant would tell him where it had been sent.

He stood up and began down the only path that led out of the room. As he reached the door, it swung open without him even touching it, and he passed by the sapphire and aquamarine bushes. As he passed by them, his anger burned inside of him at the thought that both of them hadn't bloomed, like all the others, since his rule began.

As he exited the room, the door closed behind him, and he began to walk up the stairs. These stairs were narrow, winding, and actually led to his private quarters on the third floor, so it was a long climb.

The climb always gave him time to ponder what was going on and to plan a course of action. Even after being put through his torture methods, that Dathen boy had not been any more helpful than he had been the two nights and single day previous. Not only that, but the boy didn't even survive the methods and died before he could become of any use.

"It is so hard to find good help," he voiced, frustrated.

This, however, didn't help, and he continued his trek up the stairs with only torches to light his way. Then there was the matter of his brother, who was more useless than that boy and hardly as loyal. With Constance by his side, there was no way he could be trusted.

Exotius was the other issue. He was powerful, and there was a chance, however slight, that he could overthrow the king. This was something he was always on the lookout for, and since the visit to the House Made of Trees, he was going to pay even closer attention.

His thought had carried him to the landing and the secret door in front of him. As it opened before him, he found himself in a grand bedchamber and watched as a framed portrait came down and the bookcase closed behind him. His room had gold-plated trim and a balcony that looked to the west, where the great lake of Veteris Spiritus resided, along with the ancient ruins of Aquamarine.

There was a grand fireplace across from his king-size canopy bed, which had drapes of red mingled with black. There was a set of furniture that the people of Earth would call chairs and a sofa; he just called them furniture. There were wood end tables with gold inlay in the shape of untamed flames. The door located directly across from the balcony led to the hallway to his private floor. The rooms on this level were off-limits to those without his personal permission.

There was a library, a study, a second bedroom that was never entered, and a dead-end with a balcony facing the north and the royal garden. The hall led to a staircase that took him to the second floor, where special combat training was taught. Then it continued down to the ground floor, where there was an entrance hall, a throne room, and a ballroom. Not to mention that there were several bathrooms on each floor. The second floor led to another staircase, where there were guests' quarters and the larger and more public library. The dungeons and torture chambers were located below the ground level, and a hallway just to the right of the main entrance led to prisoners and people like them.

He grinned to himself. He had just taken a mental tour of his own castle, but that was fine by him because he knew every nook and cranny in this castle: every secret passageway, major and minor room.

As his thoughts fell on the castle's floor plans once again, a knock happened at the door.

"Sire," the voice of one of his guards echoed, "Exotius and your brother, Jonathan, are in the throne room."

Say what? he thought angrily. How could they be back so soon?

"Very well," he growled.

With those words he heard the guard turn and leave to return to his position at the end of the hall.

Those two had better have a damn good reason for returning so quickly. After all, he hadn't minced any words with them. They knew what was expected, and if they haven't at least gotten the girl, there would be hell to pay.

Deciding he better go down, he pulled on a shirt and walked toward the door and opened it. As he walked down the hall and down the stairs, he was setting his mood for when he entered the room. He decided that he would pretend that he was curious before he lost his temper. At the bottom of the stairs, he arrived in the entrance hall, and here he veered right down another hall, passing a few minor rooms and then stopping at the door on his left.

When he entered the room, a man announced his arrival, and the two men performed a low bow as he walked past them. When he finally sat down on his throne, he turned his head in order to look at the men in the room. His fierce gaze practically told them that they had best have a good reason for showing up without Heartington's daughter or the youngest son of Tungston.

"Well," he said, putting on a false smile, "this is a surprise. Here you both are—"

"Sire—"

"I'm not finished," he said, and at this point, he was on his feet and walking toward them. "As I was saying, I am surprised. And it seems that you two are the only company I'll be having tonight."

"Igneous." Jonathan winced.

"Yet," he pressed on, now only feet away, closing the gap fast and completely ignoring his brother, "I distinctly remember saying that neither of you were to return without bringing to me the last of the Heartingtons and the youngest Tungston."

Here he paused, letting his words crash upon them like a storm-driven wave would upon the shore.

"So," he growled, with all pretense of understanding and generosity gone, replaced only with rage, "I hope that one of you will have a very good reason for being here and disobeying every one of my very direct orders!"

His voice was now reverberating off of the walls and ceiling, making the last of his anger-driven words echo for a few moments after he had finished. As he stood breathing very heavily, he found himself looking into the eyes of both men. He found them to be displaying very different things.

In his brother Jonathan's eyes were complete and utter terror and a clear wish that he was anywhere but in this room, which was just about normal. Exotius, on the other hand, was a much harder read. Igneous's best friend and man had eyes that hid all thoughts and emotions, but his overconfidence sometimes gave away what it was he was thinking.

"Sire," whispered Exotius, with an attempt at shame in his voice, "I admit to failing you."

"Oh, I already knew that!" Igneous raged, "I just haven't guessed how yet!"

"If you permit me, Your Majesty, I shall explain," Exotius said calmly, "but know this beforehand: Jonathan and I plan to set things right, no matter the cost."

With raised eyebrows Igneous walked back to his throne and sat down and waited for the story to begin. Exotius explained about the traitor in their midst that he had disposed of after he had found the escape tunnel. He learned of how the lion Jerard had been an explosive magical device that had led to the deaths of five men. Then he heard about the cave collapse that had stopped them in their tracks and ruined all. How getting back he had come out of a tunnel in HawThorns, and after heading to Decorus Regnum Corset, he had run into Jonathan and Constance at the gate to the city.

Here Jonathan explained his intentions to rendezvous with Exotius to help look for the girl. Jonathan admitted that he had seriously considered waiting for his brother to return up at the castle but had thought better of it and was about to set out toward HawThorns when he saw Exotius approaching him. That it was at the gate of Decorus Regnum Corset that both he and Exotius decided to wait for the king to return.

When they were done speaking, both men stood before him, waiting for him to pass judgment. He could most definitely tell Jonathan was speaking the truth and assumed that Exotius was mostly doing the same. If it was all true, the rebels' hideout must be in the Forest of Magus or Promise. Wherein they would be even harder to find, and he had already decided he would rather defend his city against them than go and find them. As for not getting ahold of the girl, now there was no question of what would be done if she were found; she must be destroyed.

"Sire?"

Exotius had spoken first, clearly wanting new orders or some other form of direction. However, it was at this point that something distracted him from Exotius by walking into the room unannounced, and it was white.

Constance, he thought irritably, just what I needed right now.

"Welcome, Constance," he said with a smile on his lips but with a tone as unwelcoming as his eyes. "I see you managed to miss my lecture on disappointment once again."

"*Oh*, I am disappointed," Constance said sarcastically as she came to stand next to Jonathan, "I was *sooo* looking forward to it."

Igneous's mouth twitched at this. Exotius had placed one hand over his eyes and was shaking his head.

"Constance," Jonathan hissed, his whole body shaking, his face blotchy. "Shut up!"

At these infuriated words, Constance stretched out her front legs, extending her paws and claws, and she opened her mouth in a long, toothy yawn.

Igneous scowled and stood back up. There was much to do; he needed to start looking for the Tiara and had been in high hopes about having the girl out of the way by now. But that was not the case, and now it more critical than ever to find the headdress first.

"We need to move quickly," he was saying more to himself than to the others. "If the girl finds the Tiara before us, we will be at the disadvantage."

"Why?" Jonathan said ignorantly. "I mean, it's just a piece of jewelry. It couldn't possibly do anything for her."

"Idiot!" Igneous shouted, his temper at full boiling point, sending Constance crawling for cover. "The headdress is an icon to these people. Whoever has it will be considered the rightful ruler of this kingdom."

"OK!" winced a cowering Jonathan.

"Where would you like to start, my king?" Exotius said with fire dancing in his eyes.

"We will start by researching every possible place that it could be." Here he paused to glare at them both. "Then you and I, Exotius, will go to search the most likely of the places while Jonathan stands guard over the castle and the city."

"Igneous, I don't think I could—"

"Where he will lead part of my army in defense of this city, or he will suffer my ultimate and unwavering wrath!" Igneous had shouted this last statement and had, in doing so, drowned out the rest of his brother's sentence.

He was tired of his cowardly brother leaning on him for protection. What probably aggravated him even more was that his brother Jonathan's animal, Constance, had more of a spine than his brother did.

"Now," Igneous said in a very forcedly calm voice, "I want to see you both in my private library in one hour's time *and* for you to be ready to work until we find all of the answers."

With these final words, he looked at his brother and Constance who, at some point, had decided it was safe to come out from behind one of the many pillars. Both she and his brother looked weakly at him at the sound of the word "work." For Constance it was simply a lack of drive; she just did not want to do anything that required her to produce an end result. For his brother it was for a different reason. Jonathan hated working with his brother because Igneous was a very hard man to please.

Exotius simply gave a small nod and began to walk around the room, looking at one of the paintings. For him it was just another day of serving the king.

Satisfied that he had been understood, he began to stride across the room. Just as he exited the room and was about to continue left, he heard Exotius start to speak to Jonathan and decided to lean on the wall and hear what he had to say.

"See, I told you that if you remained silent, he would believe both of our stories and not just mine." It was with these words that Exotius began to walk in the other direction, slightly chuckling an evil chuckle.

"I don't think," Jonathan whispered slowly to Constance, "that my silence is why Igneous believed me, or him, for that matter."

"Why do you say that?" she whispered and began to clean herself.

"Because I know Igneous, and he has never been fooled or been made a fool of."

"He was both, twenty-one years or so ago," Constance mused as she continued to clean herself.

"That," Jonathan said in a tired tone, "was a onetime thing."

And with those words, Jonathan began with Constance in the same direction that Exotius had gone. It was only as his brother's footsteps had faded that Igneous went left down the hallway and began his trek back to his private wing. He made most of the journey back without thought. It was as he began up the second flight of stairs that he couldn't help grinning to himself and saying aloud,

"At least you know me by now, my brother."

CHAPTER 17

Training to Be Rose of RTET

Camp of RTET, Forest of Promise

It had been more than a week since Rose had arrived in the Forest of Promise, and some changes had come about in her. Some were noticeable, like her appearance. The clothes that she had been wearing since she had arrived were now torn, stained, and just plain filthy. She was now wearing a set of what seemed to be generic armor. It was all black, and man, was it hot and heavy. She was still wearing her boots despite many objections by the people equipping her. The armor was not the only addition she had to her appearance. She was now equipped with a sword, shield, and a bow with a sheath of arrows, all of which she was expected to master.

The other differences were not as noticeable, and this was because they were internal differences, differences that were conflicting with everything she had previously known. Things she was still trying to tackle with all that was taking place. Depending on the day, she would catch herself feeling confident about how things could work out in the end. Then there were moments when she felt that these people were piling all of their greatest hopes onto a dead horse.

Remembering that she was supposed to be watching James and Liam, who were trying to teach her the great art of sword fighting, she came back to the match before her.

"Now, Rose, watch me and Liam."

She had to admire James, who was so confident that she would get things right in the end.

"James, I think we should start her off easier than this." Liam was having a hard time voicing his opinion, as he was doing so as their swords and shields clashed, and he seemed to find himself almost not ducking in time.

Valor, who was standing next to Rose on her right, had his water-like eyes on the two men.

"James," his crisp voice rang, "you're straying from the original formation and are about to lose."

Rose watched as James quickly refocused on the task at hand and was finally concentrating fully on what he was supposed to be doing. This was bad for Liam who, while James was seeing if Rose was paying attention, had started to gain the advantage in the match. Then with spectacular speed, James disarmed Liam and forced him to the ground by grabbing hold of his forearm and flipping him.

"I yield!" Liam cried quickly and slightly nervously, as James now had his sword pointing directly at Liam's throat.

"That was very well done," said the calm voice of Enigma, who was the animal that belonged to Liam.

Enigma was a great gray wolf; his fur was almost silver, however, and from his lower jaw all the way to the tip of his tail and extending all the way to his paws, he was a pure white. Yet his eyes were so gray that they were almost black.

"Liam," he continued in his deep, calm voice, "you need to focus more. I can tell that your mind is elsewhere."

"What?" Liam said in a slightly agitated and distant voice, "I don't know what you mean, Enigma."

"Never mind," Enigma said, shaking his head as Liam sat down beside him and then focused his gaze on Rose.

"I thought you did rather well," Rose said jealously.

"It was not his best, though," James said concernedly. "Liam is the head of the weapons division, and usually his skills are almost equal to mine."

"So I'm having a rough day!" Liam shouted at him.

"You don't need to get all hot and bothered!" James replied just as loudly.

"Well here you are criticizing me when you have no idea what I'm going through!"

"Oh, I think I have a pretty good idea, you overconfident—"

"That is enough, both of you," came the deep, slow voice of Valor. "By fighting with each other, you are inspiring little to no confidence in your leadership capabilities or your friendship with each other."

"I agree," came the deep, growling voice of Enigma.

Both animals were now watching their respective humans as they breathed heavily and stared at one another.

"Sorry, James," Liam said in a slow, tired voice, one hand rubbing the back of his neck. "I think I just need some time to myself."

"Sure," James said apologetically, "I understand."

With that Liam and Enigma left the part of the clearing they were in and started toward the village of tents. This just left James and Rose together, as it seemed Valor wished to go graze someplace a little quieter a few yards away.

"So," James said, and he turned and looked at her, "ready to give it a try?"

"I don't know, James," she said unsurely.

"Come on," he smiled, "what is the worst that could happen?"

"You might cut my head off." Rose smiled before continuing to say, "I'm sorry, did I say 'worst'? I meant best."

With that she picked up the heavy shield and sword and tried very hard for the next few hours to gain some form of advantage over James. She didn't even come close.

"You're getting better," he said with the smallest of smiles, and when she looked at him in complete disbelief, he followed with several more votes of confidence.

"James," she said with a great sigh and groaned as she sat down on the ground, "what you are asking of me is almost as difficult as controlling the night sky and all the stars in it."

"Rose, come on, you're—"

"James," she said, cutting him off and standing back up just as he sat down, "I'm tired. I think I will go to my tent and go to bed."

"OK," James quietly said in a sad voice.

As she was walking away, she heard Valor start to whisper to James. She was sure that it was probably about her. Why not, she thought, I mean, I am making a complete fool of myself in everything people are showing me.

There were several "hellos" muttered as she walked by, but they were halfhearted. When she had arrived, people were excited, thrilled even, but she expected that she had turned out to be a great disappointment to most of these people.

"I can't even stab someone when I am right next to them," she hissed angrily to herself.

She was mad because to kill was just not in her for some reason or another; she just could not do it. She was now passing through what would be a village square if there had been buildings here and not a massive amount of tents. She went left toward a larger tent she shared with Aphra, Topaz, and Vengeance. She had been given a quarter of it in the back. She happened to like her corner because it had a flap that came down and gave her some much-needed privacy.

"Hello?!" she called, relieved when no answer came.

"Good," she muttered, "peace at last."

She continued to the corner and pulled down the flap. In her space was a nice little cot, a chair, and a small desk with a few candles. Quills and parchment were lain neatly on it, but she had no need for them.

She walked over to her small cloth bag and pulled out the painting. The bag was magical; she could put as much as she wanted in it, and it would never get full or be heavy.

She carried the painting over to the cot and sat down, holding it before her. It looked so real, and the painter had been set on the notion that this headdress had been of a very simple and delicate design. It *was* beautiful, she thought, but I am not worthy of such a thing.

How could she rule these people, who were more talented and sure of themselves than her? She couldn't even defend herself. How could she defend a people who were born able to defend themselves?

She got up, put the painting back in her bag, and sat down at the desk. She wanted to write a note simply saying "Sorry" and leave, but she just couldn't do it. With sadness and helplessness settling in, she changed her clothing and blew out the candle. She then lay on the cot and began to cry herself into a restless sleep filled with war, death, and a faceless king.

CHAPTER 18

Normal Hopes for Turbulent Times

Edge of the Camp of RTET

L iam Draughtningr was sitting on a stump facing the southwest and thinking about the city of Decorus Regnum Corset and the people living there: namely one woman in particular.

This woman had deep, long auburn hair and big, warm brown eyes. She was not very tall and had a frail-looking form with pale, smooth skin. She wasn't frail, though; she was as tough as they came and a Cryptic Conspirator for RTET.

Her name was Rachel MacNeil, and she was the woman that lived in his best dreams and haunted his worst nightmares. She was his fiancée, and they had decided to keep their love for each other a very deep secret.

No one knew of their love for or their engagement to each other except for two other beings: her cat, Damien, and his wolf, Enigma.

"Your mind is not here." Enigma had been so quiet that he had managed to get right next to Liam without him noticing.

"You're mistaken," Liam said quietly and continued to look in the direction of the woman of his dreams.

"No," Enigma sighed, "no, I don't think I am. You are thinking about her again."

"Yes." His answer was distant.

"You wish you and she were together."

"Yes."

"Yet you both agreed that it was best to wait until everything was sorted out before coming together as one." Enigma's eyes were on Liam, who seemed to be on the verge of just getting up off of the stump he was on and going to her.

"We agreed to that years ago, and now…" He gazed longingly. "Now I wish we had just continued through with it and accepted the consequences."

"You did the right thing," Enigma said quickly and sternly. "Had you been together, the king's people would have gone after her when he discovered you as part of the plot against him."

"He may still harm her, should she be discovered spying for us." Liam's eyes were filled with a pain known only to those who loved deeply. His fists were clenched, and his face was wrought with worry.

"I know how you feel, Liam."

The voice had come from behind Enigma, near the path that eventually led to the Pool of Hope. As they both squinted in the moonlight, the figure of James Tungston formed as he approached them.

"James!" said an appalled and infuriated Liam, "How long have you been there?!"

"Long enough to know that if I stayed there longer, I would risk hearing the name of the woman you miss and fear for."

"Why lurk in the shadows, James?" Enigma said calmly, his eyes never wavering from James's, "Why were you listening in on a conversation that was not yours to hear?"

"Yes," Liam said quickly and pointing a finger casually in his direction, "why were you listening to us?"

Liam watched as James looked toward the camp, a sad, longing expression on his own face. He seemed to be lost, either in thought or in feelings. When he finally spoke, his voice was cracking, and his face had become rigid.

"I was sitting and thinking about how I was going to grapple with the situation that I am in." His face now turned away from the camp and back in the direction of the Pool of Hope.

"What kind of situation?" Liam said, sort of bemused. "It's not like you, like the rest of us, didn't know what we were getting into. I mean, we all took the risk."

"I do not think that is the situation to which he is referring," Enigma said concernedly. "James, is there something on your mind? Something that is bothering you?"

James looked at the two of them and seemed to be deciding whether or not he dared to tell them whatever it was that was bothering him. Liam was almost completely sure that he was going to keep his secret to himself when James began to speak.

"Have you ever wondered what it would be like to betray the one you loved to the cruel twists and turns of fate? To do so after you removed them from a place where fate's hand could not deal them blows as horribly as it can where they are now?"

Here he paused and looked them both in the eyes. He seemed to be searching for his answer there. He got none.

"Well I have." He winced slightly and looked up at the now star-filled sky. "When I first met her, I was determined to get the job done. To do what needed to be done. Then I learned more about her and began to spend more time with her. The more I learned and saw her, the more I began to fall for her."

As he paused once more, Liam knew who he was speaking of.

"Rose was not like any woman I had met. She was honest, couldn't lie to save her life, and noble; she told me she would never kill, even if she had to." James took a deep breath and continued. "I knew in the end, she would be no match for the king, but it was my task to make her believe that she could be. To believe she could take down a bloodthirsty, vengeful tyrant."

Here Enigma's ears drooped ever so slightly, and Liam's face had become very pale. What James was saying was that the person they had been waiting for may be little to no help to them at all.

"I left her to be free, and when she was brought here, I was faced with the same horrible predicament." He looked at them again and then redirected his gaze to the stars. "That I would have to help train her and most likely help her into her deathbed."

"James," Liam swallowed and continued, "you must realize that she *is* the one who is meant to free us, our people, our world."

"But at what cost!" James half shouted, half groaned. "What is to become of her in the end!?"

Liam was about to answer when Enigma spoke first.

"You love her, don't you, James?" Enigma whispered.

Liam waited for James to answer. At first it looked as though he wouldn't or he expected the stars to give him the answers. Then after a few moments, he spoke.

"More than the life that courses through my own body," he said, practically collapsing to the ground and covering his face with his hands.

"Then if this is the case, you will be sure to let nothing happen to her," Enigma said calmly and with visible confidence, "nor will you allow anyone you do not trust to come near her. You will guard her with your life, as you do with Valor and he does to you."

"James," Liam said carefully, "don't you see that you are what fate has handed her?"

"How do you mean?" James asked, confused.

"I mean you are everything she is not," he continued, his own problems as distant for now as the stars themselves. "You will help her become what she needs to and make up for what she cannot become."

"James," Enigma said, sitting in front of him and placing his right forepaw on his knee, "we will help you stay strong."

James first looked into Enigma's eyes and then looked up at Liam. Nodding, and without saying a word, he got up. He then turned to them and said, "And I will help you stay strong."

Liam looked into the brown eyes that were suddenly filled with fire. Then, when it was clear there was nothing more to say, James began to walk slowly back toward the camp and appeared to be thinking to himself.

"Liam," Enigma whispered, "she will be there when we are victorious."

Liam knew that it was not Rose they were talking about anymore; it was Rachel.

"Liam," his voice was even quieter than before, "I bet she is the one that saves us all."

Liam smiled. He then thought, And we will hoist up the new flag together.

CHAPTER 19

The Decision

Center of RTET Camp

ose was trying her best to get herself together before she exited her part of the tent. She had skipped breakfast and avoided Aphra and Topaz this morning when she went to get washed. Upon her return, she noticed that both women and their animals had left.

She was supposed to work on her archery skills today, but she was not feeling up to it. She wanted nothing more than to be back in her and her father's shop, getting those bouquets ready for that couple that was getting married soon.

She stopped by the mirror and took a look at her reflection. She looked, at least on the outside, like she was ready for anything; calm and collected was how she presented herself. She was wearing her armor once more. However, she had decided to wear her hair up in a tight and intricate braid. Inside, she thought to herself as she stared into the mirror sadly, I'm ready to run away screaming and to throw caution to the wind.

"Rose?"

It was Valor. He always seemed to be coming to get her, practically pushing her out of the tent.

"Rose?!" Valor called out, exasperated, "I know you're in here somewhere."

"I'm coming." She sighed and took one last look in the mirror to make sure she looked presentable. "Just keep your shirt on."

As she came out, he looked at her strangely, and if he had been human, she firmly believed that he would be scowling at her.

"I do not wear nor have I ever worn a shirt," he said deeply and followed her out of the tent, shaking his mane as a woman would toss her hair to right it after it had been messed up.

"It's an expression," Rose said, rolling her eyes. "It means the same thing as 'give me a moment' or 'hold your horses.'"

Valor gave her a penetrating stare, and after passing in front of her as if to make a point, he then began to walk in front of her. He was leading the way to their destination and taking them away from the center of the tents: first by taking a right and then by taking a left once they had passed all of the remaining tents.

There wasn't really a path that led to the archery training ground, but they were easy to find, as they were located on the very edge of the clearing. It was actually more on the edge than she realized, as she observed that it was almost in the forest. Different trees were marked with targets, which she knew were used to test skill and accuracy.

"Good morning, Rose," came the slightly growling voice of Enigma. "I hope you are well rested and ready for today."

"As ready as I'll ever be," Rose muttered with a halfhearted smile on her face. Inside she was terrified. She had done so poorly in everything else that now she felt this sense of desperation to do well with this particular skill.

"Rose." This time it was Liam that spoke, and with a wave of his hand, she caught on and walked right over and stood beside him. "Rose, we will be practicing archery today. I am going to show you how to assemble and disassemble a bow, how to hold it, and how to load the arrows. Also, I am going to show you the proper firing stance."

"OK," she said, praying she would at least do this well.

He spent what would be the equivalent of an hour explaining the different parts of the bow and how they worked, how to assemble it and, most importantly, how to load it correctly and efficiently.

After all this he asked her to take her stance; once she did he poked and prodded her into what he called the "appropriate" stance, but what she called the "most uncomfortable" stance.

"I can't shoot like this!" she cried out at him, all the while barely staying in place.

"You're going to have to, because that is how it is done," Valor said, lying there and speaking in a matter-of-fact way.

"It will get easier as you get better," growled Enigma.

However. it became clear very quickly that she was no better at archery than any of the other skills she had approached.

"You are trying too hard, Rose," came Liam's voice, but it felt very distant, separate from herself.

She was exhausted and tired of failing at everything in this world that she tried to do.

"I think I would like a quick break, Liam." Rose said quietly, and she carefully made her way toward Valor and sat on the grass near him. Once on the ground, she brought her knees up and placed her chin upon them, wrapping her arms around them.

"Why don't I do things well?" she sighed, speaking freely now that Enigma was engaging Liam in a conversation separate from her own. "I mean, I am trying, and I think I understand, but—"

"There you go," said Valor, casting her a calm glance. "You think but you are not sure, are you?"

His eyes pierced her own, and they said nothing for a while after that. It was as they sat there that a young man with a tough build and blond hair approached Liam. The man spoke to him quickly before turning very abruptly and leaving.

"I wonder what that was all about?" Rose whispered to Valor, craning her neck to watch the man leave. Valor cast her a strange look that seemed to say, "I know, but I will not tell you because I can't." After turning his head in another direction, Valor seemed to decide he had better be leaving.

"Hey," Rose said, slightly nervous now, "where are you going?"

"I think I will go and see if I can't find out where James is today," he said without breaking his stride or turning his head.

"I thought you said you knew where he was earlier," Rose called after him, agitated, and now fear was slowly filling her heart and soul. Her fears were far from eased when Valor seemed to pick up his pace and didn't even answer her.

"Rose," Liam was speaking to her and was now only a few yards away and closing the gap fast, "we need to talk."

"All right," Rose answered in an unnaturally high voice; she found herself placing her hands on her hips. Why did I do that? she thought and quickly lowered her arms into a straight position at her side.

"Rose," he sighed and looked up into her face before continuing, "I was just told that the day after next there will be a sort of send-off happening."

"For whom, or…" Here she paused and saw Enigma, who was now sitting where Valor had been, was staring at her unblinkingly. "Or for what?"

"Well it's going to be a kind of celebration for you," he continued, now turning away and walking toward the edge of the forest.

"What kind of celebration?" Rose breathed. Her heart seemed to be on the verge of stopping, and her mouth had gone drier than the desert.

"Well…" Liam hesitated, and before he could continue, Enigma began to speak.

"It is a send-off celebration that is given whenever a human enters the Forest of Promise in search of their destined animal." He looked at her and must have been watching as the blood steadily drained from her face in terror. "After the celebration you will enter the forest and begin your search as everyone wishes you luck."

"You guys are joking, right?" she asked hysterically, looking quickly between the two of them. "I mean, you're just trying to motivate me."

But one look at the two of them told her that they were being very serious, and that a lack of motivation was not the reason why the told her. Her heart was sinking farther and farther into her stomach, and her mind was racing.

"Rose?" Liam had put his hand on her shoulder and was looking concerned. Her silence was clearly worrying him.

"I'm fine," she said in a hollow voice.

"Are you sure?" Enigma said, his eyes reading her thoughts, it seemed, once again. "Because if not, talking about it could help."

"I'm fine," she replied, no more convincing this time than the last. But she brushed Liam's hand off gently and turned to look at him. "Really. I just need to go to my tent and, um…think."

"OK," Liam said as she walked away, leaving them at the edge of the clearing.

She was moving very quickly, and her mind seemed to be going just as fast as her feet. It would be humiliating to have all those people watch her. Not only that, but she wouldn't even measure up in the end the way they expected her to.

Her fears had carried her to her tent, and she quickly ducked inside. It was midafternoon now, and people were busying themselves elsewhere. With a quick glance around the space, she bolted to her corner and grabbed her bag. She wasn't going to stay, wasn't even going to leave a note. This was not her world; these were not her people, and she was not their leader.

With these final thoughts, she exited the tent and made her way to the southern edge of the camp, in the direction of what she knew to be a pool of water.

"I will fill my canteen there," she said aloud, but there was no one around to hear her. No animals or humans came down this way much, as there was a small well at the northern end of the camp, just beyond the clearing.

"What does that matter?" she said out loud once more, disgusted with herself for saying anything at all. She trudged through the heavily wooded area.

It took her most of the rest of the day's light to reach the water on the other side of the trees. As she reached the water's edge, the sun was resting on the treetops, about to sink down. Well, she thought, it is beautiful, with the great trees and the island reflecting in the water.

Wait! she thought, An island?

Right in the middle of the pool, an island had suddenly appeared and couldn't be larger than a quarter mile in any direction. Not only was it small, but it was heavily forested with trees that seemed to be growing with every breath she inhaled as she stood there. It was also perfectly round, and that in and of itself was odd.

She hadn't realized it, but in the water she was now almost standing in, there was a small bar of sand appearing before her. She almost tripped and fell upon it in absolute shock. It seemed to be leading directly to the island's shore.

She knew it was probably stupid to think that this island appeared solely for her, but she did. It would also be incredibly stupid to cross the sand bridge and go onto an island that could just as suddenly disappear as it had appeared.

"However," she sighed, "maybe home can be found on that island."

And with that, she placed her right foot on the sand and then her left; she looked both ways to see if someone was watching. Then she began to run across the mysterious bridge of sand, so as not to have a chance to turn back.

CHAPTER 20

Wasted and Well-Mapped Time

The House Made of Trees

E xotius stepped over the broken form of Jasmine Traymeda; in his own opinion, she had long ago outlived her usefulness. The musty, earthy smell of the house was now mingled with the smells of his struggle with her. The smells were of sweat, blood, and death; it was a mixture that he was very familiar with.

King Igneous was standing in her private quarters, an area to which she would always retreat to when she was through talking to whomever it was standing in the main room. Speaking of the main room, he thought; he took a quick glance around the corner to see what was transpiring.

Men that were a part of the king's personal army were actually at that very moment tearing through the room. They looking for an object that wasn't wider than most of their hands and was far thinner than anything they had ever come in contact with. They were instructed, however, to take anything useful back to the horses for safekeeping.

"Exotius," Igneous called from the other room. His tone was that which belonged to a man who was less than pleased. Not that he was very often, Exotius thought.

"Coming, sire," Exotius called back and thought, as he answered, that they had done fairly well, considering the circumstances. He took one final look at the men to remind them of their job, should any dare get distracted, then he turned and began to walk in the direction of the king's voice. He continued to think about their good fortune as once again he stepped over the old woman's body and headed toward her private quarters.

After all, he told himself, they had been in luck when Traymeda's animal, Indifferens, was nowhere to be seen. This bit of good fortune meant that the old woman had no warning about their coming. Apparently, he thought, smiling an evil grin, she didn't have that bit of foresight telling her about someone's imminent arrival.

He continued to smile as he relished the expression on her face as the king came barging through that door, Exotius with him and a small army in his wake. His smile then widened as he thought about how foolish she was to believe that she wasn't expendable. Everyone was considered expendable to the king, including himself. Here he paused and found himself standing outside of the doorway of what seemed to be Jasmine Traymeda's bedroom.

Inside on the left and all the way back, there was a small four-poster bed, whose frame had lost its brilliant finish and drapes many years previous, it seemed. There was a second fireplace that was directly across from the bed, and on the back wall, there was a small window that was, he thought, curiously open. Pausing, he thought, *That is odd for such a cool night.* Near the fireplace was a worn wooden stool and matching table. They both only had three legs but were square, as opposed to the traditional circular style.

"Are you going to frame yourself in the doorway or come here?" Igneous muttered coolly and with an air of impatience that was clearly meant for him. He looked up and placed his eyes upon Exotius, those eyes that could burn.

"Sorry, sire," he said humbly, but meaning not a word of it as usual.

"No, you're not," the king said unsmilingly and beckoned him over to the wall nearest the bed. "Come take a look at this."

Exotius did as he was told and walked over to the wall. Here his jaw might have dropped if he were the kind of man that would reveal his emotions. The wall had been converted into some kind of hand-drawn map. The map was very detailed and depicted what was considered the most populated parts of Aquamarine; it even included titled locations and a compass.

"Well," he said, taking a closer look and running his hand over it, "someone had a lot of time on her hands."

He turned to look at the king and then said,

"Why do you suppose she took the time to do such work?"

Igneous ignored the question and began to move closer himself, so close, in fact, that he now stood only a mere foot away. He then stretched out a hand and began to gesture at the faintest of markings hidden under the labels.

"These old markings that are faint and barely readable," he said, pointing to a part of the forest near the House Made of Trees on the map, "they are the same everywhere."

"Yes," Exotius said, looking slightly amused, "the words are 'Not Here,' whatever that is supposed to mean."

"It means this was her way of keeping track of where she had looked for it," the king said in a hushed and disgusted voice, and then he, too, ran his hand over it.

"You mean to say she was searching for the tiara too?" Exotius exclaimed, having to work very hard to remove the shock from his voice. "This whole time she was trying to get the upper hand on you, my king."

"Look over here," he said without so much as acknowledging Exotius had said a word. "The Mountains of Treachery, the Mendacious Forest, Lake Veteris Spiritus, and Ancient Aquamarine. They are all marked 'Not Here.'"

"Those were the places we were going to search," Exotius grumbled coldly, his mouth twitching ever so slightly. It aggravated him that one week of doing nothing but research now had them no closer to finding that foolish headdress.

"What about HawThorns and the Forest of Promise, sire?" Here they both took a look at the map and saw the same two words.

"Well it must be somewhere," Igneous said with utter fury filling his cold eyes. Those eyes looked to Exotius as though they were made of fire.

"What about here, sire?" Exotius asked, still looking at the map and pointing at the House Made of Trees. Meanwhile Igneous went over to the fireplace and stretched out his arms, placing his hands on the mantle; his eyes were now resting on the dancing flames.

"It doesn't say that it's 'not here.'"

Still gazing at flames, Igneous seemed to be carefully thinking about his answer.

"She wouldn't be looking for the tiara elsewhere if she already had it here," he said through gritted teeth, and his face had hardened.

"What if this is just meant to fool you, sire?" Throwing his hand in the direction of the map in frustration. "It would be just like her to do so."

"She did not know that I would see this," Igneous said more calmly as he continued to watch the flames eat away at the smoldering logs. "She thought that I would never eliminate her, that I would always need her. She did this for her own benefit, for her own wondering mind."

"So," Exotius paused, "you think she *was* looking for it on her own? I mean really looking so as to best both sides?"

"I think she would have wanted to sell it to the highest bidder." Here Igneous looked up and stared at Exotius with a hard look on his face.

Exotius would have found such a thing hard to believe, but then again he didn't know Traymeda as well as the king. The reason being, of course, that Exotius had refused to work with her at all.

"So where do we stand?" he asked, looking into those fiery orange eyes.

Igneous, ignoring Exotius, stood straight up, and as he did so, the fire extinguished, put out by magic, though the king hadn't uttered a word. He turned and slowly made his way to the doorway and beckoned to Exotius with a wave of his hand. The two of them continued back to the main room, which had once looked organized and now looked demolished.

"We are leaving," Igneous barked at his men, who quickly got out of the building through the only door there was and out of the king's way.

Exotius followed the king outside, still waiting for a response, something he often found himself doing. The men were now busying themselves with getting ready to depart when the king turned to him to speak.

"Now we must return to the capital and prepare for a fight that is sure to come." He paused and turned back to look at the House Made of Trees. "I think it is safe to say that the tiara is a legend and nothing more—at least to these people." He finished this sentence with a gesture of his hand.

"What makes you say that?" Exotius said in an undertone, still facing the men; which was a good thing, as two of them were now preparing Wildfire and Infestus for the long ride ahead.

"Because," the king smiled, "if Traymeda couldn't find it in all her years of looking, it can't possibly exist, at least not out here."

"What do you mean by that?" Exotius said, bemused. It was like the king was insinuating that the tiara was in the castle or something.

Annoyed, Igneous turned to look at his top man with a glare that would send most men running—most men.

"If it isn't here, then it must have been hidden in plain sight somewhere: somewhere I wouldn't think to look." He hissed this sentence, continuing to hold Exotius's eyes in a piercing stare. "What better place than within the very walls in which I live? The place is so enormous, with plenty of nooks and crannies in which to hide something very small."

"If you say so, sire," Exotius said, leading the way to the horses and mounting Wildfire.

"I do," Igneous said smugly, mounted Infestus, and started to lead them toward Decorus Regnum Corset when a crackling noise came from behind them.

"The earth is sucking us in," Infestus cried, but Igneous forced him to turn around and see what was happening.

Exotius, who had not yet moved, now watched as the House Made of Trees sank into the ground from which it came. It appeared that it had not been nature but magic that had created this strange form, and the magic holding it had died with the old woman. The roots seemed to be like ropes, as they were now pulling the tree carefully down. It was done so gracefully that it seemed to look as though it was the most natural thing in the world. Then it was gone. The clearing in which it stood was now simply a clearing with no reason for existing at all. The trees that were great and always seemed to be full of life were aging before their eyes and now seemed old and dead, giving the clearing a haunted aura.

"Well," said Igneous, calling his shocked and stunned men back to themselves, "I guess we won't worry about anyone finding her, will we?"

No one answered.

CHAPTER 21

Heartington Castle

Heartington Castle, Decorus Regnum Corset

Constance was lying on her canopy bed, which had curtains of red, and the wood that formed it was of a charred nature. The bed was set up in a small room that was connected to Jonathan's room. It was most likely a nursery originally, she supposed. But what it once was really didn't matter to her, because now it was hers. The room had no windows, so therefore it was lit by torches, but she knew that it was, like Jonathan's, facing the Mountains of Treachery. It was also in one of the highest parts of the castle. This room was one of her favorite parts of the castle, as it was quite secluded.

She lay there, admiring the many tapestries and the few paintings that filled up the room. They were old and were among the few things that had survived the king's purge of everything that had been connected to the Heartington family.

One thing in particular that would enrage the king if he had known of its survival would be a shield with crossed swords that held the Heartington family crest upon it, which was now hanging over her fireplace. The crest had a great winged unicorn in the center, with its head turned to face the onlooker. The unicorn was standing behind a single rose that seemed to just be opening and still held all of its thorns upon its stem.

"Constance!"

That will be Jonathan, she thought, who probably had just found all his papers on the floor. He was probably quite angry due to the fact that he had ordered her to close the balcony doors and she hadn't—yet. It was her opinion that he had servants for that. I mean, she thought, stretching her front paws and slowly getting up, *Why should I have to do such things?*

"*Constance!*"

Ugh, she thought, he was such a different man after he has spent too much time with his brother. He had a tendency to get twitchy and irritable, and it would take very little to send him over the edge.

"*Constance!*"

"I'm coming," she purred calmly but made her way slowly into Jonathan's room, looking up at him with what would be considered by most as a blank and innocent expression.

Jonathan's room was far larger than hers and far grander. It had a great balcony facing the mountains and a large fireplace with his family crest held just above the mantle. Across from his fireplace was a great canopy bed with a frame that was intricately carved with dancing flames. The only similarity his had to hers was the charred nature of the frame and the red curtains; everything else was far more exquisite.

He also had a bathroom with a grand bathing area in the floor made out of stone, a washing basin, and a mirror, which she was forbidden to use. His room included some furniture, two intricate wooden tables, several candelabra for special occasions, and two large sitting areas with furs leading from there to the bed area.

His high ceiling was framed in gold leaf, and held in its center, a great amber chandelier. It would magically illuminate when darkness came, and it would extinguish whenever someone wished them to or if the sun was coming up.

Now her attention came back to Jonathan's less-than-pleased face. Instead of his more cheerful and playful clothes, he was wearing what Igneous would expect him to. He was wearing a shirt that was black and high collared, with red embroidery throughout the cuffs and edges. He was also wearing the black pants to match, with black boots that came up almost to his knees.

"Constance," he breathed coldly, "is it possible that you misheard me? Or did you just feel that I was speaking to the walls surrounding me?"

"I thought that you meant 'eventually,'" she said lazily, noting that his mouth had gone thin and was now twitching. "I didn't realize that when you told me to close the doors, you meant right then and there."

Jonathan's face went red, and he turned on his heel, took several long strides toward the balcony doors, stretched out his arms, and slammed them shut.

"Constance," he said very quietly as he turned around to face her, "let me make something very clear: my brother expects me to keep this place running the way he likes it while he is gone."

He paused, and as he did so, he walked so as to stand right in front of her.

"Which means you are expected to *share* the duties *we* are responsible for." He looked into her eyes and did so unblinkingly before continuing. "That includes, but is not limited to, following orders, defending this castle and this family's beliefs."

"So raping, murdering, pillaging, and destruction to promote fear," Constance growled. She never much liked being scolded for something as frivolous as this. After all, she was not a servant, and now that she thought about it, she had picked him out, not the other way around.

"If that is how you read it," he replied nonchalantly, looking out at the mountains before turning back to look at her, "then yes."

As if this conversation resolved the matter, he turned and walked into his bathroom. Here he took one look at himself in the mirror, and he strode over to the door leading to the hall. Turning toward her, he then smiled and said,

"By the way, I would very much appreciate it if you would pick up my papers."

With that he opened the door and exited the room, practically slamming the door behind him.

"Well," she said huffily.

This was not at all like him; he was usually very mousy with her and didn't normally dare to tell her what to do. That being said, however, they didn't normally stay here. These two rooms usually remained unoccupied due to the concept of remaining out of the king's hair. They thought that the best way to do so was to remain at the Stipes' summer home as opposed to staying here, where Igneous terrorized them.

Sighing, she glared at all the paper on the floor. Technically it was parchment, but somehow the word "paper" had leaked into this world from that other one. Deciding that grabbing the documents and placing them in their proper place would be wiser than ignoring Jonathan a second time, she began to collect them carefully with her powerful jaws.

It took her the better part of what would be an hour to locate and carefully replace the pieces of parchment where they belonged. She had decided that since she knew the correct term for the documents, she would use it.

As she was just finishing up, Jonathan's newest fancy, also known as a maid, walked into the room with her white cat, Damien. Damien was more of a soft gray when seen next to Constance, and his eyes were an orangey gold. The maid wasn't the tall type and had long hair of the deepest auburn. Here warm brown eyes were in extreme contrast to her pale skin.

She was here to ready Jonathan's room for the evening. She had, like most of the others, volunteered to be Jonathan's maid. Probably, Constance thought, because she thought he was handsome and far kinder than his brother. She would probably sleep with him, too, like all of her predecessors. Once that happened, her tour of duty would most likely be over, and she would have to cope with everything that happened and everything that didn't.

That, Constance thought with a frown on her face as she watched the girl turn over the covers, would be if she were lucky. Someone of her beauty might end up working for Igneous next, and that was considered a less pleasurable experience. Some women didn't live through what happened with him, and those that did wished they hadn't.

Constance shook her head at such thoughts and walked past her as she headed to the balcony. She carefully opened one door by lifting her right forepaw and dropping it on the handle.

"I'll get that for you, Miss," the maid said quickly.

"I am perfectly capable. Thank you, Rachel," Constance replied coldly. After all, she thought, I am not a common house cat, or leopard, for that matter. I am smart enough to open a door.

The maid, as if she had heard what Constance was thinking, rolled her eyes and left the room. Her cat, Damien, stared at Constance for the smallest of seconds and then followed his human out of the room.

Constance rolled her eyes in sarcasm, but no one was there to notice, so she proceeded onto the balcony. Once on it she lay in the shade, enjoying the evening warmth. She had been there for quite some time when she heard a commotion down in the yard below. A bunch of horses were being led into the stable just below and to the right of the balcony.

Strange, she thought, they had left only a few days previous. Why have they returned so soon?

Maybe it is another group that has come back after going out for the day, she thought hopefully.

However, all of her hopes were crushed when she saw the black, fire-tinged hair of Exotius Obscurum below, leading Infestus and Wildfire to their private rooms that were on the ground level right below the balcony.

"This is not good," she said, a note of panic in her voice, and she was clambering to get up and over to the balcony doors. She was in such a hurry that she knocked over a potted flower as she opened the door. Once in the room, the sound of nails on glass filled it as she hastily closed the door behind her. Moving quickly across the room, she was thinking just as hurriedly,

I must find Jonathan; he'll want to know Igneous has returned.

CHAPTER 22

The Island of Destinies

The Pool of Hope

Rose had finally reached the island after running across the great sand bridge. The island, only a few minutes previous, had seemingly appeared in a blink of an eye, with the bridge forming at her feet.

"Damn," she said through heaving breaths, "that was farther than I thought."

Still breathing very heavily due to her now-winded condition, she turned and looked for the shore she had left behind. Her jaw dropped; the sand bridge was now sinking back into the water and out of existence. It was as though someone had flipped over an hour glass, and the sand was flowing into the base.

Well, she thought to herself, I guess there really is no going back now, is there? With a sigh she looked around and took in the world to which so many said she belonged. But she was not part of this world; she had come from and belonged to another world, she told herself.

With that thought still fresh in her mind, she turned on her heel, took a deep breath, and walked into the wood.

She was instantly met with complete darkness. In fact, it was so dark she could not even see the hand that she had placed out in front of her.

"How in the world am I going to see where I'm going?" she frustratedly groaned aloud.

Suddenly, as if in answer to her words, a faint greenish glow came from somewhere to her right. Turning, she saw that it seemed to be coming from a rock that was only a foot or so off of the ground.

She started to move closer to it, moving with caution but filled with curiosity. Once near the glow, she could tell that it wasn't the rock emitting it but an object sitting upon the rock. She picked it up and held it, still unsure as to what it was.

I mean, she thought, still holding the thin yet surprisingly sturdy object tightly, it's better than walking around in the dark, bumping into things. As she looked, squinting into the bright light, she saw that the source of the green glow was very small, sharp, protruding objects located in a seemingly basic central frame.

She could not get over how terribly light it was, because in holding it, she could feel how strong it was. Yet, she observed, running her fingers along it, she found the frame to be very fragile in nature. The fact that it was brighter than her surroundings meant she really couldn't see it properly. But while running her hands over it, she noticed that its shape wasn't completely circular, yet it was still round.

"Very strange," she whispered. "I would never have believed such an object as this could exist, had I not seen it with my own eyes."

Nevertheless she was glad to have the light. The object, whatever it may be, was therefore a very welcome sight. Not to mention an addition to the few things she now possessed. With it she was now able to proceed farther into the thickening wood, and hopefully her journey home would now be clearer as well. Her hopes that the island's center would hold some path back to Earth seemed to gleam in the darkness along with the object's glow.

After a while one tree seemed to look like all the others, with each being as massive as the next. They are even larger, she thought, than those she had read about growing in California. The canopies of the trees seemingly blocked all hope of natural light.

The terrain was just as tough as the never-ending darkness. There were roots the size of her legs raised above a path that someone had long ago forgotten. However, she thought, at least there is a path, even if it is strewn with boulders and roots waiting to trip an unworthy traveler.

She felt as though she had been walking forever and figured it must be daylight by now, though you could not tell since the canopy had seemed to have gotten thicker. My feet and my legs, heck, she winced as she stubbed her toe on a root, my entire body is moving in absolute protest. Her exhaustion was beginning to force her to a halt, and just as she was about to give in…

"Finally," she sighed, for there before her was a clearing.

She moved faster to reach it and stubbed her toe a few more times before doing so. Here in this clearing was a general sense of peace. At its center was a little pool of water that was no more than five yards in length, and it was in the shape of the crescent moon. Its water seemed to illuminate the darkness. Perhaps this is the moon, she thought, and I'm walking on the night sky.

"Don't be silly, Rose," she said, shaking her head at such a silly notion.

No longer in need of it, she placed the object in her bag, not noticing, however, that it had ceased glowing.

She yawned. Now that she had stopped, that exhaustion that had been slowly building up had fallen over her. Knowing it wasn't the ideal place to rest seemed to make little difference at this point, as she once again let out a wide yawn.

Slowly, cautiously, she entered the clearing and saw the only place she would find fit to lie upon. There was a little patch of grass that came to rest in the indent of the moon-shaped pool. She smiled as a memory of her father washed over her. He was drawing a moon just like this one, and there was a star hanging from its upper tip. The grass reminded her of that funny star, which always seemed to her to be holding on by a thread.

She sighed and dropped her bag on the ground next to her and sat on the grass. It was a little cool but soft as silk. She lay down fully now and curled up to keep warm. She took one last look at the pool before closing her eyes and allowing the blanket of sleep to envelop her.

"Ahhh!" Rose let out a terrified scream as she was awoken by something lifting her up and throwing her into a tree on the other side of the clearing.

"What the—"

But mere words could not begin to describe what she was now looking at.

The thing that had just thrown her was over eight feet tall and was absolutely hideous. She counted several large appendages that included two slimy, scaly tentacles; six hairy legs, three on each side of its single torso; and two clawed arms covered in hair, with three appendages each. It had two mouths on its large pear of a head, one on top of the other, and it had one very long, gray tongue.

One mouth had a pair of fangs baring at her, the other a set of very sharp, razor-like teeth. In between the two mouths, resting on the scaly head, was a pair of green eyes, with red veins pulsing through blackness that would normally be the whites. To top it all off, besides the arms and legs that were a furry dark gray, the rest of it was a black, scaly, and slimy.

She opened her mouth in what would have been a scream, that is, had any noise come out. She stood up shaking, feeling that fight-or-flight thing she had once learned about start to take effect.

The ground shook ever so slightly as the creature took a few large and clumsy steps toward her, its eyes never veering from where she stood. Its tongue seemed to be moving between mouths, licking first its lips, then its fangs.

Not thinking clearly, Rose made a run for the other side of the clearing where the path was. This, however, seemed to be in her advantage because the creature, while swinging out with its clawed arm, didn't stop in time and slammed into a tree. It was also successful, as it had sent Rose flying into the clearing and away from her intended destination.

"Ah, OK," Rose winced, dazed and standing up once more, thinking she could make another attempt at reaching the trees. She ran for it.

"*Ahhh!*"

Once again sent flying in the other direction, this time she landed near the pool of water. Quickly she rolled over and saw something utterly terrifying. There, in the back of that horrible creature's head, parallel with the other pair, was a second pair of eyes glaring at her.

"Ohhh, crap!"

She stood up and tried to get around the pool and at least get out of the creature's range, but it had turned around now and was somewhat coordinated. It swung out with its left clawed arm and got her left shoulder.

"Arrrgghhh!"

She fell to the ground and curled up for a second, groaning in pain. She started to try to get up but was pulled down again by one of the tentacles.

"Get off!" She screamed at it and kicked it hard with her free foot. It let out a horrible sound that was a cross between a roar and a wail. It was so loud she covered her ears. Then realizing it let go, she scrambled to get out of its reach.

This, however, was no longer possible, as the creature, having learned its lesson, had now wrapped its tentacle around both her legs. In fact it was almost up to her waist.

"*Help!*" she screamed; why, she wasn't sure. After all, who would hear her, let alone be a match for this terrifying creature?

The creature, now realizing it held her fast, was now slowly standing up and readjusting itself. Once it seemed to have found a firm footing, it lifted her up so that she was now almost level with its face.

It held her there, and she wondered if somewhere there was a noise she could not hear, and it was now smelling her to see if she was worth all of that trouble. Then both of its mouths opened, and it let out that same horrible cry, but this time it was in triumph. She felt her hair fly back and smelled its putrid breath.

Then it began to move. It was walking away from the clearing, away from the pool and the path she seemed to have walked down forever and a day ago. She was being swung backward and forward as if she were some toy, not a living thing.

It seemed to be heading for another clearing just to the north and west of the one she had found. This one was not very bright; the light seemed to come from tiny droplets of water that were resting on the trees and flowing into their roots.

"*Ahhh!*"

The creature had dropped her, but it noticed right away and snagged her once again with its tentacle. Lifting her once more so that she was dangling near its mouth, she struggled to get free.

It seemed to realize she might have a chance, because it then grabbed her arms with a clawed appendage and pulled her tight.

She grunted with the effort to get free and suddenly sensed that she was now out straight like a corncob before it. Then it opened one of its mouths, the one with the two long fangs, and she closed her eyes even though it had turned her so she was back to its mouth. This is it, she thought.

She let out a cry of pain as its fangs grazed her back, making two long gashes from above her left shoulder down to her right hip. Tears were now spilling from her eyes as shooting pain coursed through her. She breathed heavily and held her breath every other second. Her armor was hanging on by mere threads.

Suddenly she felt something slimy wrap around her and pull off what remained of the armor. She realized in horror that it was the creature's tongue. The creature then wrapped its tongue around her, licking her as if she were a lollipop.

She was beginning to wonder if this is how she was meant to die: being licked to death. Then it turned her around, and she knew that she could only be so lucky. The creature had brought its tongue back in and opened its second mouth. This mouth had many large, pointy teeth, and the tongue had come out once more. This time it wrapped tightly around her and was starting to pull her toward the teeth. She closed her eyes, expecting excruciating pain, when she was dropped to the ground, right on top of the armor.

"Wha..." she moaned slightly and rolled over to see why.

It was letting out an ear-shattering wail, and Rose saw, though her vision was quite blurry from blood loss, that a strange, black form was repeatedly stabbing the creature.

Rose decided that she didn't want to be this new arrival's dinner either and ran back to the clearing of the crescent moon pool. She wobbled and staggered until she reached the edge, but having lost so much blood, she couldn't go any farther, and she passed out. Her form toppled down a small incline until it came to rest near the pool's edge.

Her last thought was that the creature had obviously lost its meal to a far hungrier and more aggressive creature, and that this new arrival was sure to make it impossible for her to ever wake again.

It was only as Rose passed out that the black creature appeared next to her. It was a great black unicorn with wings. The creature lowered its head and nudged Rose's form. It then raised its head, and its golden horn glowed white hot, and Rose was raised a foot off of the ground. Walking behind her, it moved over to the crescent-shaped pool and lowered Rose into it.

Rose's head rested on the bank. Her body was floating almost level with it, as if she were a fallen leaf. The creature then lowered its horn toward the pool, and just as the tip touched the water, it began to glow white as the moon. Rose's wounds stopped bleeding, and her face regained the slightest amount of color.

It seemed that the magic had only worked slightly, for the creature frowned and raised Rose out of the pool shortly after putting her in. It laid her on the same patch of grass Rose had fallen asleep on only a few hours previous and seemed to be waiting for her to wake.

CHAPTER 23

Nightsky

The Island of Destinies

"Rose…" came the voice of a woman. It was warm, soft, and calm. It seemed to be coming from thousands of miles away. It was the only thing drawing Rose from her unconscious state and back to a world of reality and pain.

"Rose," came the voice again.

It was high. But not too high, she thought. What was even more perplexing was that the voice knew her name.

"Rose," came the voice clearer than ever, and it seemed louder too.

"Wake up, Rose," it coaxed. "You're safe now. Wake up."

She stirred and felt the reality of it all hit her hard. There was pain in every inch of her form, and it was particularly bad in her back. Knowing she could delay it no longer, she opened her eyes to find the heavens directly above her; the canopy of trees had parted slightly to reveal the starry sky above.

It took her a few moments to realize that she was lying next to the crescent-shaped pool where the attack had initiated. She also noticed the absence of her armor, and why was she *wet*?

"Rose."

The voice called again, and Rose turned her head ever so slightly to the left and saw four black legs attached to hooves. These legs were blacker than the blackest of nights and looked quite strong.

In an attempt to ask a couple of questions to the legs, such as: *Why am I wet?* and *Who are you?* all she was able to manage was a gargling noise. It seemed that her extensive injuries were making speech far from possible. In fact the mere effort to do so had caused her to breathe erratically. Worse still, her back was shooting with pain with every breath that she took.

"Rose, you mustn't try to speak," the voice replied to the gargling. "I've done all that I can here by placing you in the pool and coursing it with a healing magic."

Rose turned her head to look to her right at the crescent pool and then closed her eyes.

"Rose," that beautiful voice whispered, "we must get you back to the camp."

"No," Rose moaned and shook her head very slightly.

"I'm afraid we must," the voice whispered in a sympathetic way. "You need proper medical attention, something I cannot provide."

Wincing, Rose opened her eyes and stared at the sky.

"I used the pool to attempt to heal you completely, but the magic coursing through your veins prevented me from doing anything but stopping the bleeding."

"If I go back, my problems will only multiply," Rose said, finding her voice through her fear, but it came at a price, for each word she spoke tore at her chest. Each breath, her lungs. She didn't even react to the utter nonsense of there being any form of magic in her at all. If she was meant to die, she wanted to do it right here. Why would she want to move to somewhere else and cause herself more pain just to die there instead of here?

"Rose!" The voice was no longer sweet and musical, but harsh. "You are going back. As for your other insecurities, I will help you with those as we encounter them."

Then there was the sound of some sort of weird wind. It clanged and jingled, as if it were putting away something metal in an already-full bag. Rose was thinking about asking what was going on when she was lifted as if by an invisible crane and onto the back of what felt like a horse.

But it can't be, Rose thought to herself. Horses don't have wings. "Well this thing does," Rose said to herself, and she rolled over only to be even more uncomfortable lying on her stomach. She had only just wrapped her arms around what must be a neck when her stomach gave a lurch as the creature took off in sudden flight.

They rose higher and higher, and the canopy gap widened slightly so that they could fit through and closed just as the creature's final hoof passed through it.

"Ahhh," Rose sighed in relief as the cool dawn air fell on her face and her pain-stricken body.

116

Her vision had cleared slightly, and she could now make out, though barely, the island far below, and despite being exhausted was shocked by what she saw.

The island was sinking back into the water, and the Pool of Hope was as tumultuous as if a storm was raging over it. But as soon as the creature she was flying on made an abrupt turn toward the camp, Rose saw the water turning to glass once more.

"This must be a dream," Rose said, clenching her hands around the neck of the creature, who stiffened. "This is all a dream. Soon I will awake in my bed above the store, in my apartment."

The creature didn't respond. It just glided toward the clearing, near the center of tents where people and creatures alike were now gathering.

"Almost there," it said. The calmness of the voice had returned.

Rose saw the ground getting closer, the tents getting larger, and people moving to get out of the way. The landing was hard, and she almost felt worse now than she had all night; she was relieved when the creature finally halted.

"There," it said, slightly breathless, as if it had held its breath during the landing, "you're safe now."

That's a matter of opinion, Rose thought miserably.

"Rose!"

It was James. She didn't know why, but his voice seemed to relax her. His arms, now lifting her up off of the creature, made her feel secure, made her feel safe.

"What happened?!" came the voice of a less-than-calm Valor, from somewhere near the winged creature.

"Liam. Don. Devin. Go and get the girls. Tell them to come and help me," James ordered, not caring that he was ranked lower than one of them.

There were several grumbles of agreement as James continued to walk and was starting to enter a tent. He walked a few more paces and stopped to lay Rose down.

"You're going to be OK," James breathed, and before Rose fell into a dreamless sleep, she could not help but feel that he was speaking more to himself than to her.

Rose started to stir just as the daylight begin to fade. She was feeling quite sore and felt the tight bandages around her midsection as well as her legs.

"Rose." It was James who looked exhausted, and his voice was hoarse. He had the look of one who had gone without sleep. He had the dark shadows of an unshaven face and tired, bloodshot eyes.

"Rose," he whispered and slightly stuttered, "how are you feeling?"

"Sore." She groaned as she used her elbows to prop herself up.

"I would imagine so," he half laughed and smiled slightly. "Those injuries would have put some of the best of us out of business for at least a few days."

"They're not that bad," she said defensively, and she couldn't help but feel that he was overreacting slightly.

"You are a tough one," he said, standing up and stretching.

"What do you mean by that?"

"Well," he sighed, looking at her as she sat up now, "you just survived a fight with a trasicore, one of the most dangerous and deadliest creatures on the planet."

"I had some help in that department," Rose said, throwing her legs over the side of the bed. "Some creature killed it as it was about to bite me in two."

"Yeah, I saw that you had made a new friend."

"Whatever do you mean by that?"

"Well…" Here he paused and stood over by the entrance to her section of the tent and watched as she began to put her boots on and attempt to stand up. "This creature hung around after it brought you here."

"Really?" Rose said as she struggled to keep herself erect after standing up. After swaying for a moment, she looked at James's shocked face. "What!?"

"Well, I thought maybe after all you have been through that you may want to rest."

"I just spent the majority of the last two days passed out." Rose said determinedly, "I think I have had enough of the resting for now, thank you."

"OK," James replied with a quizzical grin.

"I suppose that now that I am awake, you'll want me to go back into that forest and find my animal."

"Actually," James grinned, "I don't think that will be necessary."

"You don't!" exclaimed a shocked Rose.

"Nope."

"Why?"

"Why don't you come and see for yourself, Your Royal Stubbornness?" James smiled and opened the flap that led to the main room of the tent.

Rose gave his backside a very dark look indeed, but he was too focused on leading her out of her room to notice her glares. He was leading her to the center of the tent, where Valor was now conversing with a great winged unicorn.

The unicorn was black, as black as the hair on Rose's head, with a horse's body that was of a strong but elegant build. The head of the magnificent beast was topped with a gold horn and held a pair of, penetrating gold eyes. The creature had a set of great feathered wings that were spotted finely with silver dots. The creature as a whole looked as though it had fallen from the nighttime sky and into existence.

"Rose," Valor said in great surprise, "I thought that you would still be resting."

"She should be, but she is determined to not get better," James said as he walked over to Valor, where upon reaching him, he leaned against his great horse, crossed his arms, and grinned. And during all of this, his eyes never left Rose's annoyed and shocked face.

"That isn't what I said!"

"No, you're right," he said, his smile widening. "You said that you were plenty rested."

"And you are just twisting my words."

She was feeling really aggravated with him now. What was his issue, anyway? What did he care if she wanted to roam around a bit?

"Rose," came the calm voice of the unicorn, "calm down."

"*Why?!*"

"Because he is seeing how far he can push you," Valor whinnied and, after shaking his head a little, whipped James with his tail.

"Ow!"

"Be nice," Valor said, and with a final look at Rose, he made his way toward the tent's exit.

"I think, James, you should leave for a moment," the unicorn said as she took several steps toward Rose, "for I would like to speak with her privately."

"Sure." He shrugged, walked over, kissed a steamed Rose on the cheek, and followed Valor out of the tent.

"Now that he has left, I can ask a question and get a truthful answer," said the unicorn, who turned its head from the entrance and back to Rose. "How are you?"

Rose couldn't help but take notice of the gentle and genuine concern in the creature's voice.

"I'm OK," Rose said, half smiling and making an attempt at a shrug. This was not, however, a good idea because the action led to a shooting pain that forced her to sit down.

"You do look much better."

"Thanks," Rose said in a disagreeing tone and looked at the beautiful creature before her. "You are gorgeous."

"Thank you." The unicorn bowed its head slightly while closing its eyes in thanks. "So are you, in your own individual way."

Rose, though she tried to think of something, could find nothing to say to that, so for a while they stood there in silence. In their undisturbed silence they listened as both man and beast walked back and forth past the tent. It was Rose who first found the nerve to restart the conversation.

"Why did you save me?"

"Because," the unicorn, which Rose had decided must be female, said softly, "you are the human that I am destined to aid in life. The one I am meant to be a partner to and be friends with. To not save you was to rob myself of a worthy companion and counterpart."

"How can you have possibly known that just by looking at me?" Rose cried out, exasperated, and sank onto the floor, or in this case the ground that was imitating the floor. "I mean, you came across me in one of my worst moments."

"What better time to judge you than in the moment where you would prefer not to be?"

Rose groaned and placed her head in her hands and shook it. How could this great and powerful creature find anything worthy to itself in a woman who was running away? This made no sense.

"You are too hard on yourself, Rose," the unicorn said and nudged Rose's head with her nose. "There are qualities that I could see past the ones I know you must be focusing on at this moment."

"Like what?"

"Before our journey through life is over, I assure you, you will know." The unicorn nudged her again, and this time Rose looked into those brilliant gold eyes. "Maybe even sooner."

"You say all of this as if you know me," Rose said, tears welling up in her eyes, "but you are honorable where I am not. You see, I was running away that night. Why, after doing such a thing, would I still be worthy of you?"

Rose looked into those knowing eyes and couldn't help but think that if she could, that unicorn would be smiling. It was as she looked back at the tent's entrance that the unicorn spoke.

"If you felt worthy of me, then worthy you would not be, Rose."

After these words, the unicorn used her snout to bob Rose's head slightly to get her to smile.

"Now," the unicorn said, "why don't we head outside for some healthier air?"

"All right," Rose said, and in uncrossing her legs, she began to stand up. She dusted herself off a bit and looked at the magnificent creature before her. Then without a second's thought or hesitation, she wrapped her arms around the unicorn's neck. In response the creature dropped her head so that its lower jaw was resting on Rose's back.

"What's your name?" Rose asked as she pulled away and started toward the tent's entrance.

"Nightsky."

CHAPTER 24

The Horrifying Discovery

Heartington Castle

*R*achel MacNeil was going about her duties as a maid for Jonathan Stipes, the younger brother of the tyrannical king that she, along with many others, was trying to overthrow. For she was more than she appeared. She was a Cryptic Conspirator, and while she looked harmless enough to a passerby, she could kill as quickly as any other assassin.

However, the position she had taken, or rather, volunteered for, had not turned out as useful as she and her fellow spies had hoped. Nearly a year's worth of work had yielded little to almost no results. And out of those few bits of information she had gathered, practically nothing had been useful.

"Rachel."

It was Damien, her white cat, and he was trying to get her attention.

"What?" she asked in a whisper, now brought back to her surroundings and the basket of clothing she was carrying.

The clothing was Jonathan's, and she was carrying it down to the wash where she would retrieve the things she had left a few days previous.

"Do you hear that?" he whispered back.

"Hear what?"

But then she did hear it. Several pleas of mercy and constant sobbing coming from the end of the hall that they were traveling down.

"That's normal, Damien." She sighed sadly at the truth of the statement. "People are always screaming down here, it seems."

She began to start up again, as it seemed she had stopped while she was listening.

"No," he said, shaking his head and taking a few cautious steps toward a hallway that was to their left. "It's coming from down this hall."

"Yeah," she said, rolling her eyes and looking up the ceiling, "that's the way down to the dungeons and such."

Once again she made an attempt to continue on her way, but Damien stopped her by standing in her way, and she gave him an annoyed look.

"Damien, people are going to get suspicious if they see us standing here chatting."

"Rachel, you've been here so long that you have completely forgotten where things are in this place," Damien said, continuing to hold his position in front of her and now making her look down the very hall they were discussing. "This hallway leads to the second courtyard."

"All right," she conceded and gave him a smirk. "So why would they be taking a prisoner in that direction, do you suppose?"

"Why ask me when you already know the rumors?"

"Yes, but that is all they are, Damien: rumors."

"Then," he said, and he jumped into the hallway, "let us go and prove or disprove them." He then began to carefully and soundlessly walk down the hallway to the door that lay at the far end.

"Damien!" she hissed.

The second courtyard he thought he was heading toward lay on the side of the castle that faced the Mountains of Treachery. But what didn't make sense to her was that the only things that were in that courtyard were the stables for the elites' horses.

"Coming?" came the loud whisper of a Damien who had almost reached the door.

"All right," she whispered back, dropping the clothing in a small cabinet that was up against the wall facing opposite the hallway, "but I'm going to stick out."

"Just say that Jonathan wanted you to check his horse or something."

"Oh, because they won't see through that," she responded, rolling her eyes.

She had covered most of the hallway's distance during the conversation and was still walking very fast because she knew that getting caught down this way would require a seriously good story. She had finally reached the door, and while it had not been more than a minute, it had felt as though it had been a lifetime.

She placed her hand on the door and pushed, praying that it hadn't been locked behind the guards; it opened. What shocked her was that the courtyard was completely deserted.

"Where did they go?" she whispered, shocked by the eerie silence about the place.

"Should there be animals in the stables?" Damien breathed.

"There are, but they aren't making a sound," she said, noticing that a normal horse was listening hard for something.

Then there came a scream from the other side of the courtyard, and the same horse whinnied nervously as there came more pleas for mercy. The cries seemed to come from the stable that was directly across from the door that led back into the castle. The very door that they had just exited.

"Damien," she hissed, "I think that I should go back for my dagger."

"There's no time, Rachel," he said, looked both ways, and dashed across the courtyard and looked back her.

"Damien," she called softly, "I would feel safer with it."

"By the time you retrieve it, we will have lost our first real lead in all the time we have been here."

She rolled her eyes for the umpteenth time that day and ran across the courtyard after her cat, and all the while she thought about what she would say if caught. It's easy for him, she thought, but if I get caught, I could blow my cover and the operation. What was worse is that she had been nowhere near as stealthy as her cat because the long dress she wore caused her to swear as it caught on one of the stones.

"Argh," she said as she reached the stable and wrenched the rest of the dress's hem off by hand, "I hate this thing. It's always in the way."

"Well now it's not, so calm down and help me find out how to work the secret door."

"How do you know there is one?" she mocked as she began to look for one as well.

"Ha ha," he said, knowing that she knew full well that was the only explanation for the disappearance of the men.

Damien began to paw at the wall that was in the very back of the stable, expecting it to open; all the while the horse was watching intently, as if to see if he would succeed. Rachel then walked over to it and began to do something with her hands, but whatever was meant to happen clearly didn't.

"This is turning out to be a pointless waste of time," Damien hissed in frustration. "There must be a way…"

Here he stopped because Rachel was tugging on the only harness in the room.

"Oh, come now," Damien snorted and sat down to watch her, "you can't possibly tell me that it is that obvious."

"It isn't," she said.

"Then why bother to…" But he was forced to stop because she gave him a dirty look that meant "Shut up."

She then grabbed the harness tightly and pulled herself up on one of the beams to the roof. In steadying herself she then used the toe of her boot in a notch that was just above the harness.

Then, with a soundlessness that could only come from being created by magic, the wall opened. It opened as if it were a double door made of stone, and it held itself there, waiting for the entrant to come forth.

"So how would they reach it, then?" Damien asked in a hushed voice.

"I believe that it is the perfect-sized notch for a sword tip," Rachel replied.

"And as no one in this place doesn't carry one…" Damien stopped at the look on her face because he realized that she would have brought hers if she had her way.

"We should move before we are spotted," she whispered.

It was with these final words that they began to carefully enter the descending staircase before them.

"Wait," Rachel said and then looked down at Damien, "I think that maybe you should stay out here, in case I need to get out."

"How will I know it's you?" he said, his eyes widening.

"I'll tap the wall two times quickly and then three times slowly," she whispered, placing her right foot on the first stair.

"I don't know, Rachel," he said nervously.

Suddenly there were voices that could be heard from down below. It was going to be now or never. Damien quickly jumped to the side of the stable and mouthed to Rachel, "Be careful." She gave a quick nod in return and watched as the door noiselessly closed behind her.

She took each step slowly and very carefully so as to avoid making any noise. The voices seemed to be growing louder, and so were the cries of pain. The pleas for mercy seemed to be multiplying the farther down she went as well. It seemed as though there was something that allowed for those in it to see what was coming, and they would beg for it not to come.

Once she reached the landing, which she suspected was about twenty feet below ground, she began to tiptoe, in a manner of speaking, toward a brilliant light at the end of the hall.

She stood very still and observed a group of men standing near several yards of thick glass, behind which was what must be the subject of interest. She decided to creep closer and stand behind a pillar that was nearest the group.

Once in that position, she was finally able to see the scene more accurately. In the center and nearest to the glass was the king, with Exotius and Jonathan standing closest to him. The sight of the king, however unpleasant, was not what made her skin crawl with horror. Behind the glass was an eight-foot trasicore, and it was holding onto a man that was clearly screaming his head off. But it seemed that no sound was capable of escaping the glass enclosure. This must have been the man that was led down here, she thought.

She expected to see him swallowed at any moment but watched, even more horrified as the creature's long, gray tongue became tubular and wrapped itself around the man's waist and into his pants. Here he was clearly at the point of extreme pain, and she was forced to look away, assuming that this creature was removing a vital part of this man's life.

"So this is a female, then."

Rachel was pulled unwittingly into the conversation of the men in front of her.

"Yes," was the reply, and it seemed to have come from the king himself, "A young one, though."

"Is she killing him?" one man asked.

"Oh, no," Igneous responded, sounding almost amused, "She is merely getting what she needs to fertilize her single egg from him, and once she is finished, she will release him, or if he was disappointing, eat him."

"Ah," continued the man who asked the previous question, "must be why their numbers are so low. Not enough hosts survive their appetite."

"Yes, that is a common problem," the king replied. "They think with their stomachs before all else. Only older ones are more responsible."

Rachel felt ill. What these men were discussing was sick. They were using humans to aid in the reproduction of trasicores, and it seemed that the creatures were indeed parasites, as long suspected. Her thoughts on the matter were interrupted by the trasicore releasing the man unceremoniously. As it was walking away, it placed a slimy green egg the size of a walnut on a stone in the forested area, just in range of the glass viewing area.

Two guards stood in front of a door that must lead to the enclosure, and in getting the go-ahead from the king, they went in. They could next be seen carefully removing the now limp form of the man from behind the glass.

"So I take it that a human female is needed for the second half of the process." Came a weak-voiced Jonathan.

"Yep," said a voice that came from directly behind her, and two very strong arms wrapped around her and dragged her into the group. It was Exotius, and she, having been so mesmerized by what she had seen, hadn't kept track of him.

"And I found us a volunteer."

CHAPTER 25

A Punishable Offense

Trasicore Breeding Center, Heartington Castle

"Well, well, well," Igneous said and crossed his arms, allowing a funny smile to come over his face as he looked upon the maid that had snuck in the room. "I think that she just might have a little explaining to do."

"And I think that she got here by accident," Jonathan piped in, his voice cracking, and that alone made his suggestion far from convincing.

"Then what would be your explanation for her ending up down here?" Igneous said as he went from looking at the maid to down at the floor for a moment. Then, still smiling a strange smile, he looked at his brother with one hand coming up to his chin.

"Well," Jonathan paused, looking from Rachel to his brother, clearly coming up with a story or trying to, "she…she could've been…"

"Could have been…" Igneous said, his smile widening, "spying."

"No," Jonathan said, starting to sweat, "no, that's not what I was going to say."

"Well that is what I believe she was up to, and I doubt you can provide a better explanation." Igneous grinned and privately believed that Jonathan's story most likely wouldn't even sway a small child, much less a group of grown and experienced men.

"She most certainly didn't get here by accident." Exotius groaned while holding the woman fast while she struggled. "She was standing over by that pillar for quite some time before I decided to do anything."

Igneous began to look her up and down. She was quite pretty, but not his type, although she was very spirited and fairly strong. She was doing pretty well at giving Exotius quite a hard time, and that said quite a bit for her and how strong she was.

129

"What is your name, my dear?" he asked her while examining his hands, and in looking up he watched as she tried to figure out how to best answer him.

"What do you care, if you're going to feed me to that thing anyway?" Her voice was determined, and her eyes cold.

"Maybe if I like it, I won't do as you say I'm going to." He looked at her, smiling evilly, his eyes on fire. It was, of course, a lie, but she didn't need to know that.

Jonathan seemed to seize an opportunity and stood close to his brother to speak. In fact he was standing closer than he would usually dare to.

"Her name is Rachel," Jonathan whispered in his brother's ear while Igneous continued to look at his hands, "Rachel MacNeil."

Igneous knew his brother too well to be fooled by the caring appearance his brother was presenting at the moment. He was just trying to keep open his opportunity to be with this maid and share an intimate moment. He knew that if Jonathan had already gotten what he wanted from her, this conversation wouldn't be happening. Too bad for Jonathan; Igneous didn't care.

"Rachel," Igneous said quietly, thoughtfully. Now that name did seem familiar. Where have I heard it before? he thought.

"You wouldn't, perhaps, be Danny MacNeil's sister, would you?" he said and was at last looking into her eyes in a very pointed manner. He smiled once more as he watched the anger build in those usually warm brown eyes.

"You leave my brother out of this," she said slowly, her voice shaking with anger along with the rest of her.

"Oh I would worry about him, if I were you."

"And why is that?" she said. Her voice was pure venom.

"Well, I don't think he needs you to worry for his safety anymore," Igneous said, taking a step toward her as most of the men cleared farther away from the four in the middle. "What do you think, Exotius?"

"No," Exotius said as he continued to struggle with her, "no, I wouldn't bother."

"Yah," she said as managed to elbow him, causing him to let out an involuntary breath and causing Igneous to chuckle slightly, "and why's that?"

"Because I already killed him for committing treason."

Igneous watched with pleasure as Rachel went white and as her face filled with an angry shock. I relish moments like this, he thought. Because he knew better than most that everyone has something to lose.

Her stunned nature finally allowed Exotius to regain control of her and gain the upper hand. He now held her fast. Though she tried to, she now had no chance of breaking free.

"Now," Igneous said, closing the rest of the distance between him and her, "I think that it is time that I confirm something I have thought for quite some time."

Now standing inches before her, he pulled out his small dagger. He then grabbed ahold of her left arm and gripped it tight with his right hand.

"If you wanted to hold my arm, all you could've done is ask," she said smartly, continuing to glare at him.

Smiling but not gratifying her taunt with an answer, he used the dagger to cut off the sleeve of her dress. There, exactly where he thought it would be, was a circle with a dagger-pointed *T* in the center.

"That's what I thought," he said, scowling, releasing her arm, and putting his dagger away. After being sure Exotius had her in a good grip, he walked back toward the glass.

"She's a spy!" Jonathan cried out in shock and fury, "She's been using her access to me to report on you!"

While he had figured that Jonathan hadn't had a clue, Igneous didn't share his brother's shock. The fact that his brother was shocked didn't even surprise him. He knew that Jonathan didn't usually see the signs for anything, even the most obvious things.

"How did you know?" Jonathan said, now stabbing her with his eyes.

So much for having my brother as her ally, Igneous thought.

"She gave herself away," he said softly, still staring through the glass. He was waiting. He knew that he needed to wait for just the right moment.

"How do you mean, sire?" one of the aids asked, and in order to answer and to best make his point, he turned around.

"Because she requested to be Jonathan's maid," he said, and he looked right into her eyes as he did so. He wanted to see her recognition when it came time.

"So?" she said, clearly missing the point, and he smiled at her, unsettling her slightly.

"Yah, Igneous," Jonathan said, clearly confused himself, "that really isn't uncommon."

"Perhaps," Igneous said, "but how would she know that Jonathan would be better to serve than me on her first day here?"

He continued to look in her eyes. He could tell that she was starting to get nervous now. It was as if she knew what her mistake had been even before he said it.

"You weren't even here long enough to hear the rumors and gossip about me or my brother." He paused once more to take a few steps closer to her and stare into those brown eyes now streaked with terror. "So the question became, what kind of spy were you? And while all I had were suspicions, I knew I was right."

He was once again standing inches away from her and held her gaze unwaveringly.

"I was paying very close attention to you, sweetheart, and just waiting for you to mess up."

He turned his back to her and returned to facing the glass and listened to the mounting silence behind him. The tension, he could tell, was growing, along with the suspense.

"You were careful though," he said thoughtfully and looked through the glass at the enclosure.

"I couldn't even begin to find a way of catching you." Here he paused, and his smile reflected in the glass; he continued, "Until today. Just think, you almost informed on me and got away with it."

He turned and faced the now-white form that was Rachel MacNeil. She clearly knew that something awful was coming her way.

"Almost," he said again, and he turned back toward the glass. While staring through the glass, he fingered for Exotius to move near the door to the enclosure.

She began to fight once more, but Exotius was going to have none of it. He had taken care of her worthless brother and had no quarrels with taking care of her. He reached the door and was about to open it when Igneous held up a hand and shook his head.

"Not yet."

"Oh, changing your mind, are you?" Rachel said coldly.

He couldn't help but smile and give her credit for being as she was with him. Not many men would be this way with him, let alone a woman.

"Rachel," he said and watched as the trees just in range of the glass shook very slightly, "tell me. What do you know about trasicores?"

"Not much…what does it matter?"

"Well, I've spent many years studying them. Learning what they like and don't like as far as habitat. How big the males will get compared to the females." He paused and looked at her, "What they prefer for food and at what times of day."

His eyes narrowed as he stared through the glass and smiled as he saw the trees shake a second time.

"I've even learned the answers to the age-old questions and superstitions passed down to us as a people."

"Yay, and what are those?" she said snobbishly.

"I've learned that females must mate with a human male in order to produce a fertile egg. That no other animal can be used as a substitute."

Pausing, he turned away from the glass and started toward her while pulling out his dagger once more. With a swift movement that would be missed if one had blinked, he made a thin cut the length of her tattoo. He squeezed her arm and watched as it began to bleed.

"I have learned that the females will be more likely to attack a human female than a male, and vice versa." He watched her and could see his inference of what was to come start to take effect. She knew what was coming.

"Do you know much about Earth's black widow spider?"

"Say what?" She looked at him as if he were nuts.

"Earth has a spider called the black widow, and it is quite deadly," he said as he walked slowly back to his position by the glass. "The female has a tendency to eat her mate after performing a reproductive action."

He saw Rachel out of the corner of his eye and could tell that she was revolted. But it wasn't just her. Most of the men behind him didn't find the concept too appealing either.

"Like the spider," Igneous continued, unfazed by the concept they were discussing, "I've observed that females will more likely than not eat their partner after mating, but that males have a tendency to keep their human host for future use."

Here again he looked at the woman Exotius was preparing to throw into the enclosure to allow her to learn firsthand about the creatures they were discussing.

"That is, unless they were a complete failure as a host or if the creature gets really hungry."

He walked over to her for what he expected to be the last time and stood before her.

"I would have warned you not to go up against me," he said, looking into her eyes and smiling, "but I would think that a warning wouldn't be necessary."

Still smiling, he patted her cheek before finding his place before the glass for the last time. He saw what he had been waiting for. A ten-foot male trasicore walked into view and spied the egg. Quickly it scooped it up with its tongue and hid it away on the inside in what Igneous could only assume was a special pocket somewhere in its tongue.

Turning his head, he nodded at Exotius, who in turn nodded at the two guards posted near the door. The guards opened the door, and Exotius pushed Rachel in. Another guard who had found her cat, Damien, sent it in after her. Then they locked the door. Rachel must have ordered her cat to get out of the way of the creature, because those watching couldn't see him.

"As you can see, males have a sense of smell that is far better than that of the females." He was saying this all while the trasicore wrapped a tentacle around Rachel's left leg and pulled her near him.

They all watched as its tongue wrapped around her waist and went up her skirt. With them all standing behind him, it was almost like Igneous was giving a lesson to a group of individuals that had come from far and wide to hear it.

"Males insert the egg inside the woman very carefully with their tongues and will make sure that they are properly placed."

Unlike the female trasicore, the male that was holding the woman in front of it had turned away from the viewing area halfway through the process and now held its back to the group. Igneous felt in some ways that he was being robbed of the sight of seeing her scream her head off.

The rest of the men in the room shifted uncomfortably, with the exception of Exotius. He, like the king, continued to stare unperturbedly and was unmoved by what was happening.

"It is at this point that having two sets of armlike appendages comes in handy, because he will use one tentacle to hold the woman and the other to keep the egg in place. This leaves the other two appendages free to catch other food."

Igneous paused and waited for the beast to put the woman on its backside and wasn't disappointed. She was now being held against its back, and he continued his lecture.

"The tentacle will keep the egg in place for the duration of the incubation process."

As they all watched what was happening, he heard one man in the back being sick at the sight of it. They all watched as the creature, with the woman in tow, left the viewable area and disappeared from sight.

With the show over, Igneous turned around and faced the men in the room.

"It will take up to fifteen days for the young trasicore to hatch, at which point the male will feel it and pull it out. If the male should wait too long to do so, however, he could kill the female host when pulling it out because the young trasicore will be too large. Once it is out, and should the host survive, the male will stick its tongue down the host's throat and drain three-quarters of the host's stomach acid. This is used to feed the young trasicore its first meal. After which the young creature will leave, for fear of being eaten, and will live off of smaller animals until fully grown."

Here he watched as the men in the room were speechless. He knew that all the men in the room now knew one of the penalties for treason and would never commit it themselves. Nor would they allow any woman they cared about to commit it either.

"If the incubation is successful, the trasicore will more likely than not keep the host for the next mating season," Igneous said and smiled.

He then turned around and started through the group of men and toward the direction of the staircase. He didn't even stop until he reached the archway that was at the end of the room. He turned around and motioned for Exotius and his brother to follow him. It took them mere minutes to catch up and wait for him to continue. He looked at the others and simply said,

"Dismissed." And he smiled as he passed through the archway and left the room.

CHAPTER 26

The Battle Plan

Heartington Castle

*I*gneous had just left the viewing room of the trasicore breeding center and was walking down the narrow hall that led to the stairway. He took a sharp right and started up the stairs. All the while he was thinking about what he was going to do now that one of his biggest secrets had been discovered.

Once he had reached the door, he waited as Exotius went over to the doors and placed his sword in a notch right in the middle of the top of the archway. The door opened, and they walked through it and into the stable.

As the door closed behind them, Igneous had reappeared in the courtyard and was now taking long strides across it, with Exotius and his brother, Jonathan, in tow. Jonathan, needless to say, was angry with him for disposing of his next plaything and, to top it off, was struggling to keep up.

"Igneous," he called after him as he was about to reach the door.

"Igneous, I want to talk to you," he said with anger lacing his words.

Stopping just short of the door, he turned quickly, smiled, and said, "So talk."

"You had no right to dispose of her," Jonathan said. Daggers filled his eyes, and he was doubtlessly using them to carve Igneous into small pieces. "She was mine, and I was to punish her as I saw fit. Those were the rules that we set long ago."

"The rules have changed," Igneous said shortly, turned, and opened the door in a swift motion. He entered the very hallway that the maid must have traveled just moments before. Striding down it, he took no notice of Jonathan's repeated efforts to catch him.

He took a left at the end of the hallway and continued at a breakneck pace until, with a final turn to the right, they were in the entrance hall. That is when

Jonathan made a bold move and grabbed Igneous by his upper right arm and turned him around to face him.

"You can't just change the rules of the game without consulting the other players," Jonathan breathed. His nose flared like a dragon's would before it breathed fire.

"I didn't realize that you had decided to play." Igneous grinned and watched with extreme pleasure as his brother released his arm. He then walked over to the wall with a huge painted depiction of himself and Jonathan.

"You told me we were equals when this all started." Jonathan breathed softly, "Well, so far as I can tell, we're not. We never have been, and I think you believe that you own this world entirely, and that would include me."

"Go on," Igneous said, a dangerous look in his eyes, and his mouth curled slightly.

"Well you don't, Igneous, and I'm not going to be ordered around anymore. If you want me to do something, you best ask, because I'm about to walk out that door." Jonathan's face was dark and cold. "Don't forget that when we left Tungsten, we were running from two brothers that would be more than happy to have me tell them where you are."

"All of this because of one maid," Igneous said, walking over to a pillar and placing his hand on it.

"She was mine!"

"No!" Igneous shouted back, "She belonged to me. I just let you borrow her for a time. She was my subject!"

"You had passed her up; therefore she was mine!" Jonathan retorted, his voice rising, "You can't just change the game when you feel like it!"

"The game," Igneous said in his most dangerous voice, "can always change."

Jonathan looked as though he was about to retaliate when he saw Exotius shift slightly. He saw his arms uncross, and he now had one hand resting on the hilt of his sword.

"And if you can't change with it," Igneous said, casting a short glance at Exotius, "then you may very likely be eliminated from it."

"You can threaten me with him all you want," Jonathan said, the fire still in his eyes, "but I know that the people he pissed off are now on this planet, too, and that if I wanted to, I could find them."

"If you know what's good for you, Jonathan——" Exotius started to threaten Jonathan, but Igneous headed him off.

"If you know what's good for *you*, Exotius," Igneous said, his voice calm but his eyes blazing, "you will careful about what you say next."

Jonathan opened his mouth to say something, but Igneous shot him a dark look, and that left Jonathan silent, and he leaned against the wall, pretending his hands were more interesting. He seemed to have yielded in their fight, but Igneous knew that their fighting with each other was far from over. It seemed that Jonathan had rediscovered his spine.

"Well, now that all that has been settled," Igneous said, looking at the two fuming men, "it is time to lay out our plans for retaking this planet from her rabble."

With these words Igneous led the men back to his private library. The library was fairly large and had a great window and window seat that spanned the entire length of the room and faced the north. There was also a fairly large table where papers and maps were still lying from their last stint in here.

He walked over to the table and brushed all but the map of the castle and city aside.

"Now is the time," he said, and as he did so, once-invisible markings appeared upon the map's surface.

It showed groupings of soldiers that were located at every exit, entrance, and possible weak point of the city, with an army located at the front of the city's walls. And since he had them available, there were trasicores that where placed at the front gates.

"This is your plan, sire?" Exotius said, placing his hand on the edge of the map, and his eyes were filled with an inhuman hunger.

"Yes, but that is not the half of it." He smiled, "You will be leading the battle yourself this time."

He waved his hand across the map once more, and it showed the front gates opening and men that had once been hidden from view emerged and joined the others.

"You will have an army mightier than our last, and victory will be assured," Igneous said, his eyes afire. "Destroy all."

However, he seemed to pause for a moment, deep in thought. It was as if he was having second thoughts about something.

"What is it, sire?" Exotius asked. He was following the king's every movement.

"Destroy all except the girl," he whispered, still deep in thought. "She is mine to deal with as I please."

"But of course," Exotius said without a hint of jealousy that many had come to expect from him when it came to a massacre. For Exotius never liked to be denied the pleasure of taking certain things.

"Go now," Igneous said, not looking at Exotius but keeping his eyes on the map. One arm was across his chest, his other in an upright position, his hand on his chin. "Ready your army and set this plan into action."

"Yes, Your Majesty."

With that Exotius left the room, only to have his presence replaced by Constance, who had meandered into the room and was now standing beside Jonathan.

"So, oh Wise One," Jonathan said coldly, "what are your plans for me?"

Constance flicked her tail and held her amber eyes upon his form.

"You will remain here with me," Igneous said without a question in his voice or removing his gaze from the map.

"Why? Are you afraid I might switch sides mid-fight?" Jonathan said, an evil grin spreading across his face. It seemed to even reflect that they were related in some way.

"No," Igneous said, looking up from the map and into his brother's eyes. Then he walked past Constance and over to a book shelf, where books not of this world lay unopened for many years.

"Then why?"

"Because when it comes to fighting," Igneous said calmly and turned to look at him, "you are second only to me."

Jonathan smiled evilly and leaned against the table, his hands on it.

"That's true," he said arrogantly.

"That being the case," Igneous said, now heading to the door, "why would I want you anywhere else?"

And with these words he left the room, leaving Jonathan alone with Constance.

"So the man wants me to help defeat the enemy standing beside him," Jonathan said, his arms crossed across his chest. He looked down at Constance and snorted.

"Well, he is like that," she said, flicking her tail again. "He only notices your inner talents when it is most convenient for him."

"This isn't our world to keep, is it?"

"No," she whispered, "I don't think it is."

"We will end up going back, won't we?"

"You might." She paused and nodded toward the door that Igneous had just left through. "But I suspect he has only one more race to run, and he will be finished."

"What of Exotius?"

"What of him?"

"Do you think he will survive this coming fight?"

Here Jonathan stood up, walked over to the same shelf his brother had, and picked up a book from that very shelf.

"One can only hope that those two will get Exotius if we are to succeed in our next move."

"Do you think that those two want him badly enough to go after him and blow their cover?" Jonathan asked, looking up from the book and at her.

"They might."

"The question is," Jonathan paused and looked at Constance with inquiring eyes. "Will the brothers take us back?"

"I'm sure that they will find our story most interesting," Constance whispered.

Jonathan nodded and walked back toward her.

"However, if I were you," she said, looking up at him, "I would be more worried about her than them."

It was with those words that they were pulled into a silence. They, nor Igneous nor Exotius, would realize until later that day that Rachel MacNeil had escaped the trasicore. She had done so by using the dagger she had stolen from Exotius's belt to kill it once out of sight. The egg would be found broken in the creature's severed tentacle, and neither she nor her cat Damien could be found in the enclosure.

CHAPTER 27

The Discoveries

The Forest of Promise, RTET Camp

Since the adventure to the island she now knew to be called the Island of Destinies, Rose had greatly improved in many ways. The unicorn known as Nightsky seemed to give to her the confidence she lacked. Something else had come about, too; when trying to heal her, Nightsky had inadvertently given Rose the abilities she had lacked before. Not only that, but she had awakened an age-old magic that existed in the family's bloodline.

Rose could now shoot an arrow expertly and even manipulate it to hit the intended target when it went off course just by using her eyes. Her swordsmanship had come a long way in the few days she had been back. She was starting to defeat some of the best of them.

"You always had it in you," Nightsky kept telling her, but Rose had a funny feeling that Nightsky had something to do with it.

The most amazing thing that had come to pass, in Rose's mind at least, was that she could now run incredibly fast and was able to catch up to Nightsky without issue and then jump onto her back at a breakneck pace.

"Rose." Nightsky was pulling her out of her thoughts and back to the world. "Rose, we need to go and meet James for your match with him."

"Coming," she called back and pulled her boots on and pulled up her hair, holding it in place by putting a dagger through it. She was still using a borrowed sword and armor but was assured by everyone, from Vengeance and Nightmare to Devin and Orpheus his white lizard, that her armor would soon be ready.

"Are you excited?" Nightsky asked as she walked toward the field with Rose.

"I'm nervous," Rose replied and gave Nightsky a quick smile.

"That's good." She nodded, "It means that you are at least understanding the importance of today's exercise."

Rose didn't need to understand that; she already knew it. Today she was leading a small group of people and their animals in a battle against James and his group. They were using special swords and equipment so that no one would get more than a bruise.

"I need to win today," Rose said nervously.

"Yes, to prove you are worthy of these people who are willing to follow you."

"But I won't kill people, Nightsky." Rose said firmly, "I will do everything else, but I can't kill. It is wrong, and my father was firmly against it."

"I will help you there, then," she said calmly, walking onto the field they were about to fight on, "for I have no issue with killing those who could and would kill our people."

Rose sighed and saw her army waiting for her. She had been fortunate enough to get some very good fighters on her side. Topaz and her golden raven, Thomas, stood there with Aphra and her sapphire fox, Siren. She had gotten Devin and Orpheus, as well as Vengeance and Nightmare.

On James's team, as she had deemed it, were some real challengers, though. He had Evan and Allegiance, Don, Liam, Courage, Don's black hippogriff, and Enigma. He also had Marina Griffen, who it seemed was quite a fighter herself, and her crimson Cocker Spaniel, Comis, was a scrapper, to say the very least.

"Ready, Rose?" came Devin's voice across the field.

She gave a curt nod and started to the front of her group. There was a lot more pressure than she had expected, as she noticed the entirety of the camp had come to watch the mock battle.

"Nightsky." This was the voice of a young man holding a saddle to put on her. "I'm ready for you."

"I don't want to wear that," Nightsky said coolly. "That is made for a horse, which I am not."

"It's fine," Rose said to the young man and took her place beside Devin and Nightsky. Orpheus was next to Devin and, being a lizard of pure white, he stood out just a tad.

"Are you ready for this?" Orpheus croaked at her.

She only had the ability to nod; speech was far out of the question. She looked at James. He just looked so right on Valor, covered in his own armor and holding his sword.

"Now, Rose," came the voice of Siren just behind her, "just focus on your intended target and leave the rest to us. Don't lose focus."

"OK."

"Ladies and gentlemen." It was the voice of Pricilla Griffen speaking now. "Please keep a safe distance from the field, as this training exercise commences in three…two…"

The sound of Pricilla saying one was lost in the cries of the people charging on the field.

Rose was running toward James next to Nightsky when she realized she had forgotten her sword in her tent.

"Get ready to jump," Nightsky called from over the roar.

Rose maintained her focus and was trying to keep her panic in check. Then, just as they were about to reach James, she jumped onto Nightsky's back and felt a strange sensation.

"What the…" Rose watched as they jumped through a fiery circle that surrounded and enveloped them both for the briefest of seconds. When they emerged she was covered in solid black armor and so was Nightsky, who now wore a saddle specially fitted to her. Rose found in her hand a sword with a black blade and a very decorative handle. The shield that was attached to the saddle had a winged unicorn standing behind a rose, which had thorns upon it.

"Now we're ready!" Nightsky cried and charged forward with renewed force.

Rose raised her sword and sent James flying off Valor as he avoided her blow. She then leaped onto the ground to fight him while Nightsky kept Valor busy.

He pulled out his sword and charged her, and she readied herself for a fight she wasn't sure she could truly win.

They sent equal blows at each other that shook their whole bodies. He made a move at her head, which she ducked and counterattacked by swinging at his legs.

"Erg!" James groaned, which meant she had got him and that he would have a good bruise there now.

His fighting began to intensify, and she parried his moves but got stuck in the arm and leg in her efforts to get him. Then he knocked her sword out of her hands. She ducked and jolted out of his way, even jumped a couple of times before stepping on his sword and elbowing him in the face.

"Aw!" he cried out and kicked her leg, sending her to the ground.

"Arg!" It was her turn to groan in effort to keep in the fight. She then used her foot to trip him and get him to the ground. She reached for her sword a mere foot away, but James grabbed her leg and pulled. She kicked him, and he let go.

Scrambling to her feet, she grabbed her sword, and before he could get up, she placed it above his chest and said,

"Yield!"

"Stop!" James cried, and his whole army stopped and saw where he was. They had shock and a pleasant form of surprise all over their faces.

"I yield," James said, and he smiled up at her.

"Good," Rose panted and grinned, "because I'm exhausted."

He laughed and allowed her to help him up to his feet.

"Great job," Valor called at her as he and Nightsky trotted over to them.

"Yes, very well done, Rose," Topaz and Aphra said, hugging her for the first time and smiling. Thomas and Siren nodded in agreement.

"You have proven you are capable of doing what must be done," Enigma growled, and Courage, Don's black hippogriff, swished his tail and stared at her with brilliant gray eyes.

Allegiance and Nightmare were following Vengeance and Evan over to her.

"You did well," Vengeance said shortly.

"But you should have just killed him," Evan said coolly.

"Well you best send someone with me to do it," Rose said just as coolly, and her eyes had gone electric, "because I am not a killer."

"Rose," James said, looking nervous and standing between them, "Evan, let's just agree to disagree. OK?"

Evan just shook his head and walked off of the field, with Vengeance and their animals in tow.

"Nothing I do will impress him." Rose scowled and then turned to look at James.

"Well," he smiled and kissed her forehead, "you impressed me, and I'll follow you anywhere."

"Mr. Tungsten!" came a very high voice from near the tents. "Mr. Draughtningr! Come quick!"

The voice was that of a white, gold, and black cat, and everyone was now following it. They were led to the other side of the tents, toward the Pool of Hope, and there near the forest was the form of a female and a white cat beside her.

"Rachel!" Liam called and ran with Enigma close behind.

"Liam," she smiled weakly as he reached her, "I'm so glad to see you're safe."

"Damien," Enigma said, "what happened?"

They all sat in a horrified silence as Damien told them of how he and Rachel infiltrated a secret room in the castle where the king was breeding trasicores. He told them of the terrors that came after both she and he were discovered. He then went into an explanation of the king's ultimate plan to search the castle for the tiara.

"We wouldn't have made it if it hadn't been for Indifferens," Rachel said hoarsely. "He had found us two days ago and showed us the quickest route here."

"Indifferens?" Rose asked, full of curiosity.

"You called?" came a slow voice, and Rose turned to see the cat that had alerted them to Rachel and Damien's arrival.

"Hey," Orpheus said, clambering between feet to get to the cat, "aren't you Traymeda's cat?"

There were murmurs of agreement and lots of curious eyes straining to get a better look.

"I was," he purred softly.

"What do you mean by that?"

"Jasmine Traymeda," he said slowly with no emotion, sitting down onto his hind legs, "is now dead. Killed by the king and Exotius Obscurum. They have seen the map and know that the tiara is not in the outside world."

"What are you saying?" Siren said coolly, her fur bristling.

"I'm saying," he continued and began to clean his left forepaw, "that you are all doomed."

He finished cleaning his paw, and once finished he stood up, stretched, and began to walk away from the crowd. He continued to walk without a second look back, leaving them all in a state of shock.

"Evan." Rachel was trying to sit up, and her speech was strained. "He has a huge army. He is putting it in place right now. We have to act soon."

"We don't have the tiara though," he said, kicking the grass, his hands on his hips as he stared at the sky.

"Without it no one will rally to our cause," Aphra said gloomily.

"Not to mention," Don said coldly, "if we are caught, he may use us in a way similar to Rachel."

"We just need to stay calm for now," Rose said aloud and was just as shocked as those around her to hear how calm she sounded.

"She's right," Topaz said, her raven on her shoulder. "We can only make a plan of action if we are calm."

"I think we should all get some rest and let Rachel do the same," Rose said, surprising herself yet again and starting back to her own tent.

CHAPTER 28

Hail Rose

Camp RTET, Rose's Tent

*R*ose was sulking and couldn't help but feel completely and utterly miserable about what she had just heard.

This Igneous person seemed to be two steps ahead of them. First, he seemed to know that they were preparing for a fight. Second, he had a huge army to fight them with. And lastly, and more importantly, she thought, he knew where that stupid but important tiara was.

"Rose." It was Nightsky, and she was sticking her head through the flap secluding Rose from the rest of the tent.

"Hey," Rose said kindly, though in a sort of heavy way, and went over to let her in.

"What do you think of Indifferens's story?"

"I think that he is telling the truth," Rose sighed and went over to her desk where her sword now lay, "I wish he wasn't, but I believe he is."

"I hope he falls in a river," Nightsky whinnied and shook her head while flicking her tail. She even stomped one of her hooves to show her anger and frustration.

"That is not nice," Rose said harshly and looked into the unicorn's eyes to see the frustration.

"We'll figure this out somehow," Rose said halfheartedly.

"Yes," Nightsky said coolly, "with no help from Mister Know-It-All either."

With that Nightsky sat down next to Rose, near the desk, and watched as she examined her new sword. It was incredible, and despite the fact that it should be dented after the fight she just had, it wasn't. It was still in perfect shape and was sleek and very decorative. The handle had an emerald set in the center of the pommel. Silver inlay worked its way up from the emerald in thin lines along the grip and looked like a stem of a rose with thorns growing off it. It had a small cross guard, and in its center was a very intricately carved silver rose, with leaves completing the right and left sides of the cross guard. The black blade continued the pattern of roses and thorns.

Its black surface had a rose nearest the hilt and a vine with thorns thinning closest to the tip. It just wasn't your average weapon. To top it all off, it was so light that she could hold it in one hand, something she could have never done with the one she had been using.

Along with the sword and shield, Nightsky's saddle had come with a bow and a quiver of arrows that seemed to replenish itself at the end of a battle.

"Well, I guess today isn't a total loss," Rose said, holding the sword in both hands, an end in each.

"No," Nightsky replied, "now you and I are well equipped, and Spirorahd Eontach seems a good fit for you."

"Say what?" Rose said, shocked at what she thought she had heard Nightsky say.

"Spirorahd Eontach," Nightsky said and jolted her head at the sword as she continued, "your new sword's name."

"Does that mean anything?" Rose whispered, taking even more care now that she knew that this was indeed a unique weapon.

"Of course," Nightsky said in a shocked voice, "it means 'Of Great Spirit' in Aquamarinian."

"OK." Rose said quickly and saw that Nightsky was breathing very heavily.

They all seemed to forget that she hadn't been raised here and therefore didn't know much about the old language. Sighing, she lay the sword carefully on her desk. This act of respect seemed to cause Nightsky to relax some.

"This whole organization needs to pull itself together, or I'm going to flip."

James had just appeared from the other side of the flap and was clearly pissed off about something.

"What is it?" Nightsky asked somewhat calmly, though she was clearly still upset by Indifferens uncaring attitude.

"Oh, you know," James said, pacing and throwing up his hands, "people are freaking out. They're saying that it is over. That the king has won before we have even started. People are even discussing how to turn ourselves in, in a manner that will allow most of us to live."

"But he hasn't yet," Rose said carefully, "has he?"

"*No!*"

"OK! No need to shout!" Rose too had raised her voice.

"Well I'm frustrated!" he hollered back.

"I can tell!"

"Would both of you stop, please?" It was Valor who brought them back into focus.

"Sorry, Rose," he said softly, but the heat was still in his face, and he was still fidgeting.

"Me too." She was a little curt, though, in her response.

Rose, who hadn't realized it at the time, found herself standing and decided to sit back down. He continued to pace for a few more minutes but eventually sat down on her cot and stared at the ground. They sat there in silence for a while, he on her cot and she at her desk, continuing to examine her sword.

However, her mind was not on the sword, as beautiful as it was, but on him and how he was driving her crazy right now. She was trying to decide if she wanted to kiss him when he got up and walked over to her. And before she knew what was happening, they were in one long, slow kiss. She stood up, and his arms wrapped around her, and she placed one arm around his neck and ran a hand through his hair.

"I missed you so much," he whispered in her ear, kissing the base of her neck and running his hands down her back.

"Me too," she whispered back, barely breathing.

Then, as he took a step back, he tripped and fell on the cot, with her falling on top of him, sending her bag and all of its contents flying.

"Rose!" Nightsky cried, having been awoken from a doze she had fallen into.

"James, are you hurt?" Valor said, coming in from the other side of the flap.

He must have left at some point, and we hadn't noticed, Rose thought.

"What?" said James, smiling. They really hadn't noticed much due to the fact that they were still entangled in each other's arms and she was giggling slightly.

"I'm perfect," Rose said dreamily and watched as James smiled up at her.

"Hey, what's this?" Nightsky asked.

"It's called the start of something wonderful," James said, looking up at Rose and placing a strand of her black hair behind her ear.

"Not what you two are up to. What's this?" she said and was looking down at something that had fallen from Rose's sack and was bringing it over to the couple.

"Oh," Rose said impassively, "I found that on the island. It lit up, and so I ultimately used it to find that clearing."

James had suddenly frozen and was staring from Rose to Nightsky to the object that Nightsky now held in her mouth. He had this strange look on his face that was a mixture of awe and complete shock.

"James?" Rose was looking concerned, especially as he sat up, causing her to wrap her arms around his neck to steady herself while being on his lap. He then held out his hand as if he wanted to see it.

"Are you OK?"

"Yah," he said in a distant voice, "never better."

Nightsky, seeing the gesture, carefully placed the object in his hand, and it was as he held it that Rose got her first good look at it. It was some sort of headdress, and it had these delicate curves with emeralds sticking out in random places.

"Wait a moment!" Rose said in shock and quickly got up and ran over to grab the painting that she had saved in haste.

There it was in the painting: the tiara everyone was looking for, and yet it was there, in James's shaking hand. The Tiara of Emerald Thorns.

"Where did you say you found this?" James said. He too was now standing up and looking at her as she continued to hold the painting. He was still smiling a strange smile.

"On that island," Rose said breathlessly.

"That makes sense," he said, and he was now right in front of her, holding the headdress in both hands carefully. "Only royalty can get on that island."

"Really?" Rose breathed, but what she wanted to say next was lost as James carefully placed the tiara on Rose's head. He stood back with the other two and his smile widened.

Rose turned to look in the small mirror that stood in the corner of her tent. What she saw shocked her. She couldn't believe how closely she resembled those figures of her that were painted in James's home. It just looked normal, for some strange reason.

Then, without a hint of warning, James grabbed hold of her arm and led her out of her room, through the rest of the tent, and out of the tent, with Nightsky and Valor right behind.

"Everyone!" he cried, and they all looked at her in shock.

Rose suddenly felt very conscious of every person looking at her.

"I give you the true ruler of Aquamarine: Rose Smaragaid Heartington, for she wears the Tiara of Emerald Thorns."

"All hail Rose of Aquamarine!" Valor called.

"Hail Rose!" they cried.

Oh, you are in deep now, Rose, she thought and stared at them all.

CHAPTER 29

Following the Leader...
Wherever She May Go

Somewhere in the Forest of Promise

ose was riding Nightsky at the head of an army now ready for battle. She was now accustomed to wearing the headdress that James had put on her head only three days previous. What she wasn't accustomed to yet was leading.

Leading was a lot harder than following. It required her to always be thinking and analyzing, whether she wanted to or not. It also came with competition, as she had, in the space of a minute, kicked a bunch of people down a step. Her ideas had to have reasoning or they would be instantly shot down by Evan, who hadn't really liked her much to begin with, she felt.

Her appearance mattered greatly now. People expected her to look a certain way, and that was the biggest pain in the butt of all.

"How's it going up there?" Nightsky asked quietly and concernedly.

"Oh, you know," Rose said halfheartedly, "slowly."

"Do you want to walk?"

"Yes, please," Rose breathed in relief.

It was with that she stopped and allowed Rose to get down.

"Thanks," Rose said, rubbing Nightsky's neck for a second and, dressed in her armor and boots, she began to walk beside her.

She knew without looking that there were people behind her that had done the same. It was as if whatever she was doing was the right thing to do. It felt like some perverse game of "Mother May I?" or "follow the leader."

"Rose."

It was Evan, who in spite of her recently found situation, continued to treat her like the ground he was walking on most of the time. She almost liked him for that; at least he hadn't changed toward her because of all that happened.

"Rose," he said again.

"Yes, Evan."

"We should be reaching the edge of the forest soon," he said stiffly from atop his horse, and Rose caught a glimpse of Allegiance near him. "When we do, I think we should stop and make camp to discuss our next move."

"You think so?" Rose said, looking straight ahead and trying to stand her ground, "Because I thought we should stop just before the forest ended so that we could stay undercover."

He looked surprised, but pleasantly so, and nodded in agreement.

"I think that would be wise also," came Nightmare's voice, and Rose looked around and saw Vengeance sitting atop him gracefully.

"That's settled, then." Nightsky whinnied and shot a look at the others that meant "Get lost."

"You know how you could help me out?" Rose said, pretending to think aloud and looking at Nightsky, "You could be a little more polite."

"Bah," Nightsky replied to Rose's remark, "they are upset because they are now below you, and I am reminding them of that fact."

"Well, I need their help as much as I need yours, so please just keep it civil once in a while."

"Very well."

Rose and Nightsky continued to walk along in silence until the forest became thinner. The trees seemed to be getting younger as a whole, and light was peeking through in more and more places, casting a greenish hue along the ground. Rose knew this to be a sign that it was about to become a unforested area.

"Let's stop," she said to Nightsky, who nodded and halted.

The rest of the army slowly did the same as orders were quietly given to do so. Rose sighed, and in her head she thought, "Mother, may I stop? Yes, you may."

"I think we should stop here for now and figure out our next move while we get rested." Rose had no sooner finished when they all dismounted or began to unpack things. Tents were unloaded, and people and creatures began to erect them. Since "the big discovery," as she called it, she had acquired her own tent, but she did miss the other women with whom she had shared her last one.

Once her tent was erected, a table was placed in its center and usually would start out empty as it was now. However, within a short while, it was covered in maps and charts, even a few books.

The other thing that came to pass in all of this whirlwind was that she was frowned upon for aiding in the setup and therefore found herself standing around and annoyed.

"I'm going to see where we are," Rose said to Evan, Vengeance, Aphra, Liam, and James.

"We know where we are," Vengeance snorted in reply.

"Well I don't. And *I* want to see it with my own eyes, thank you." Rose had whispered this in a way that they all could hear her.

"I'm coming," Nightsky said ruffling the feathers of her wings and following Rose out of the tent.

"Me too," James and Valor said, setting off after them.

Rose was already trekking through some of the tented areas, where there were many "Your Highnesses" and "Ma'ams," but that came with her new situation. Some people even bowed, even though she wished they wouldn't.

"Where are we going, anyway?" James said, out of breath from catching up but smiling all the same.

"Just to the forest's edge," Rose said and looked back at him. "I want to see if Rachel's directions have proven accurate."

"Why?" he said. Clearly he was shocked by her cautiousness. "Don't you trust her?"

"It's not a matter of whether or not I trust her as a person," Rose said as she continued to walk at a breakneck pace, and they had long since left the camp.

"No," Nightsky said huffily and trotted a little forward, "it is a matter of direction."

"It falls in the same category there, sweetheart," Valor said in a quick response to her snide remark.

Suddenly and without warning, Nightsky turned right around, and Valor almost walked right into her.

"What did you call me?!"

"I said—"

"Look!" Rose called, cutting them both off and standing between two trees.

"What is it, Rose?" James said, sprinting to her side, and his jaw dropped.

There, right where Rachel said it would be, was the door to the trasicore breeding center and their point of entrance. The door had to stand fifteen feet tall, and the copper hinges and bolts had been exposed to weather for so long that they had turned a turquoise color. It was made of some kind of dark wood, and the handle was nowhere to be seen.

"Rachel said that there was a stone right at the foot of the door that would allow it to open," James whispered, and Rose could tell that he was, like her, barely breathing.

"Yah," Rose whispered.

"Yah," he repeated.

"I can't believe that it's really here," she breathed, her heart pounding. This meant that their plan would maybe work, but it was a big maybe.

"Rose," James said softly, touching her arm, "we should return and tell the others we've seen it."

"Yah…yah, you're right," she said and quickly turned away from that horrifying place.

They began walking back toward Nightsky and Valor and paused beside them.

"It will be quicker if you two ride," Valor said and allowed James to climb on top of him.

"Very well," Rose groaned. It wasn't that riding Nightsky wasn't a great honor; it was. She was just tired of riding at the moment.

"Come, Rose," Nightsky said as Rose approached her, allowing her, too, to mount her.

The journey back was indeed much shorter than the journey there, and Rose wasn't sure that was a good thing. She dismounted Nightsky and told her she could go and do what she wanted, that she would come find her if she needed her.

"Thanks," Nightsky yawned. "I think I will go and sleep for a while."

"Yay, me too," Valor said to James and quickly trotted to catch up to Nightsky and then walked a little behind her.

"I think he likes her," Rose said, grinning at James and giggling some.

"What?!" James said excitedly and smiling as if to discredit what she was saying. "No, he's just protecting her, that's all. He isn't in love with her or anything."

"Uh-huh," Rose said slyly and looked at James as they walked up to her tent, "just like you with me. Right?"

"Huh?" James said in shock but straightened himself out as they arrived at her tent.

The others had clearly been busy creating battle plans and discussing the possibilities of what could be done. The charts on the table were facing all sorts of directions, and each held a different battle plan. Each one could hold the potential of victory.

"We've seen it," Rose said and came to stand by Evan, and her voice had drawn all eyes upon her.

"Seen it?" Aphra said questioningly, her brow furrowed in frustration, and she stood straight up to get a better look at her.

"We have seen the door that leads directly into the castle," James said, looking at them all. "The one that the king most likely won't bother to guard."

"How do you know he won't?" Liam asked, looking bemused and smirking. "Where's your proof of that?"

"Our proof is in Rachel's statement about what's behind the first set of doors," Rose said, starting to lose her cool a little.

"Yes, we know," Vengeance said, rolling her eyes and standing up to get a good look at Rose. "We heard her story, but don't you find it a bit far-fetched? I mean, she was tortured in some way to make her believe that a trasicore tried to mate with her."

"How do you know that isn't the truth!" Liam said, practically shouting at her. Daggers were forming in his eyes.

"Calm down, Liam," Evan said quietly, glaring at his sister. "Keep your opinions to yourself, Vengeance, for the rest of us believe her."

"So in that case, do you believe that James and I saw the door?" Rose said coldly and looked right into Evan's eyes.

"Yes, I do," he said, and then he went from looking at her to returning his focus to the charts and maps. "I just don't know what use the information is."

"I'll tell you what use it is," she said, finding her spine and coming to within inches of the table and leaning so that she was right next to him, "We can go through that door and take them from the inside."

"I think that they *will* notice an army running into that one door, Rose," he said in a focused tone, and then he looked up at her and shook his head. "We can't all use that door."

"So create a diversion at the front and let a small group go in that door," Rose said, throwing up one hand and letting it come down hard her hip. "Find some way to get their attention so that I can get in."

"You!" they all cried in shock, and James was looking concerned.

"Yes, me, and a small party of people to help me," she said calmly with a sense of direction she wasn't used to hearing in her own voice. "I'm the one who needs to stop him. It should be me."

"Yes, but Rose, you're the only distraction that will get Igneous's attention," Aphra said calmly but looked nervous as she said it. "How do we distract him if we need you to do it?"

"Simple," Rose said shortly and looked out the tent at the tent next door to hers, which held Rachel MacNeil. "You find someone who looks enough like me from a distance and parade her around as me."

"It seems as though you have someone in mind," Evan said to her, now standing up and behind her.

"I think you should give the task to Rachel MacNeil." Rose turned from looking at him to look at them all, with her eyes stopping on Vengeance. "I think she's earned some over-the-top care. Don't you?"

"She would be a good fit, as none of them have seen you up close yet," Liam whispered as if it were a secret.

"Yah," Aphra whispered, "we could go to the front and have her lead us there. It would take a day, at most, from here."

"Once there she could act as if she were giving the orders, and they would be none the wiser," James said, grinning slightly.

"Right," Rose said and looked at the others, happy to finally have them on her page. "Then I'll enter the door that night and take them by surprise."

"I'm going with you," James said quickly.

"No," Rose said, shaking her head. "No, James, I want you to go with Rachel. It will be more believable if you are with her."

"No, I'm going with you to keep you safe."

"James," Rose said, holding back her tears, "if this diversion is to work, you can't go with me."

"But—"

"I'll go with her, James," Aphra said, patting his back.

"Me too," Vengeance said quickly, and her vote to go was backed by Evan's assurance that Don and Devin would gladly go as well.

"We will take a small group with us as well, don't worry, James," Rose said kindly, placing her hand on his arm. He looked up, and he looked on the verge of tears.

"James," Evan said in a fashion that said an order was on its way, "wake up all those not staying to go through the door. We're leaving tonight."

"Give me a minute," James replied, not taking his eyes off Rose. His stare didn't even waver as they left the tent.

"Why, Rose?" he said. His voice was cracking, and he turned away, ashamed to let her see him in this state, it seemed.

"Because," she said, choking on her own words, "it is the only way."

"Then," he said, turning around; he grabbed her arm carefully and pulled her close to him. "You must promise me that we will be together after this."

"No matter what happens, James," Rose said, placing her head and hands on his chest and feeling his arms wrap around her, "I will find you, and I will always love you."

She looked up at him, and he placed a kiss softly on her lips and let her go. He walked toward the exit of the tent, and just as he reached it, Rose knew she had to tell him.

"James!"

"Yah," he breathed, looking at her.

"I just wanted to tell you," she said, barely breathing. "I still can't believe how lucky I am to have met you."

CHAPTER 30

Across the Way

Heartington Castle, Decorus Regnum Corset

"Sire!"

Who could that be at this time in the morning? Igneous thought darkly, and he sat up. There was more knocking at the door. More like banging, he corrected himself, standing on the cool floor in his bare feet and wearing only his pants.

"Sire!"

This had better be important, he thought, striding over to the door and opening it.

"What?" he said coldly, and the guard before him jumped slightly.

"Sire," the guard breathed heavily and looked more than slightly frightened, "Exotius has returned to bring you important news."

"Really?" he said slowly and in a tone that was filled with disbelief.

"Yes, sir."

"Well then, tell him I will be right down," he said and watched the man start to run in the other direction. "Oh, and tell him if the info isn't really important, I'm going to personally torture him."

"Yes, sir," came the response, and Igneous slammed his door.

It's not even daybreak, and he was up pulling on his boots and throwing on a shirt, but he was not bothering to button it. He then entered the hallway, and he was just starting down the stairs when he was met with the less-than-pleased form of his half-awake brother.

"Why are you up!" Igneous roared, more disgusted than he had been a moment ago and now walking down the stairs to the throne room.

"Because," Jonathan said through gritted teeth, "a guard came and woke me, saying that Exotius had important information."

"So we were both awoken and are now going to meet him." This was a growling voice that had to come from Constance, whose fur looked unkempt.

"Really?" Igneous said coolly.

"Yah, really," Jonathan said huffily, "Why are you up?"

"Same reason."

"Oh, wonderful," Constance said, yawning, "someone's going to die, and the sun's not even up yet."

This statement alerted them to the realization of being at the throne room.

"Well," Igneous said, not skipping a beat and pushing the door open, "let's see if I have to kill someone before the sun is up."

"Your Majesty," Exotius said with a low bow, and he watched as Igneous, Jonathan, and Constance entered the room.

Constance bared her teeth ever so slightly at the sight of him and muttered something about it being a good thing she wasn't hungry.

"Exotius," Igneous said in a soft but dangerous voice and sitting down on his throne, "you best have a very good reason for waking me up this early in the morning."

"Sire," he said without breaking a sweat; he was clearly unworried about the king's warning. "I came to tell you that the other army is camped right across from mine."

"So?" Igneous said, feeling his temper reach its boiling point very quickly.

"Sire." Exotius was exasperated. "They are practically on our doorstep, and—"

"What is your point!" Igneous shouted, now standing and ready to grab the man before him and send him flying out of a five-story window.

"I'm trying to get to th—"

"Well then get to it, because I am this close to making you into my next empty suit of armor!" Igneous knew he wasn't being very pleasant, but he also knew he could be have been sleeping right now.

"Sire," Exotius said quietly and looking right at the king, "the girl is with them."

"*And...*"

164

"And I think she has it." Exotius stopped speaking with one look at the enraged man before him.

"What makes you think that?" Jonathan asked, looking at Exotius while leaning against a pillar. He had, up until this point, let his brother do all the talking.

"Because I saw her wearing it on her head," Exotius said in a mocking sort of way while he looked at Jonathan but then redirected his attention to the king.

"Igneous," Jonathan said, looking at his brother, who now seemed to be lost in thought, "Do you think that they had it all this time and were just waiting for her?"

"No."

"Then how——"

"She must have found it there." Igneous thought out loud and stared off into the distance. Yes, he thought, that could be the only place it could have been that Traymeda wouldn't have been able to find it. He slowly sat back down on his throne and leaned back, rubbing his chin in thought. That would explain why I hadn't found it immediately as well, he thought.

"There?" Jonathan asked, looking from Igneous to an equally perplexed Exotius.

"That island that is supposed to only appear for members of the royal family," Igneous said just as distantly, continuing rubbing his chin.

Now he had a problem. The world would know he wasn't the rightful ruler of this planet. But there is a way, he thought to himself. Yes, if he were to do that, he would be the ruler by right. She would protest, of course; she was in love with that Tungston boy, but no matter, there were ways to force her to do it.

"Igneous." Jonathan was somewhere distant and interrupting his thought process. How he hated it when people wouldn't leave him alone when he was thinking.

"Sire." Exotius was clearer than Jonathan, and now he became focused again.

"What!?" he said sharply, standing up once more.

"How do you wish me to proceed, sire?" Exotius asked. He stood very still, waiting for the right moment to ask again, if he must.

Typical Exotius, he thought, he always needs a plan and to know that what he is going to do isn't going to cost him his skin.

"Continue as planned."

"Yes, sire."

And with that Exotius left the room, knowing he was still to bring the girl to Igneous.

"You don't want him to kill her?" Jonathan asked in a shocked voice; he clearly had misjudged his brother, it seemed. Constance even looked very confused.

"No," Igneous replied shortly and started back toward the door, with Jonathan trailing him and Constance right behind him.

"But why?"

"Because now all of Aquamarine will know she has a right to that throne," Igneous said simply and continued to walk until they reached the entrance hall.

"All the more reason I would think that you would want to destroy her," Jonathan said, now climbing the stairs up to Igneous's part of the castle.

"To destroy her at this point would be foolish," Igneous said, now opening his door and, deciding it wouldn't hurt, he allowed Constance and Jonathan in.

"How so...so...sooo?" Constance yawned, showing all of her very sharp teeth.

"Because in order to hold this throne, now I will need an heir of royal blood." Igneous stopped and looked at Jonathan.

"Are you suggesting what I think you are suggesting?" Jonathan's eyes had gotten very wide, and Constance, who was lying near the fire, warming herself, was pretending not to hear a word of it.

"But of course, brother." Igneous smiled evilly. "It's the only way, and I'm sure I'll enjoy it."

He laughed at Jonathan's face and decided to finish dressing. He walked over to a door and opened it and walked in. Once in he started to put on his own armor, which was sleek and light. It was a dark ash gray, with streaks of ember red.

"She won't, I'm sure," Jonathan said, sitting down and running his hand through his hair. "She won't even want to. Won't it be harder that way?"

"I like a challenge," Igneous said, returning from the other room completely dressed and putting his sword belt on and placing the blade in the sheath. "Besides, nothing good came of something that was easy, did it?"

"But Igneous," Jonathan said, making sure Constance was asleep, for he knew she hated this subject, "she will not let you if she can help it. She most likely will die first."

"I've already thought of that," he whispered, his eyes dancing. "What if a certain young man happened to come into my possession, and she could only save him by doing what I want?"

Jonathan's eyes widened again, and then he smiled, as if all his problems had suddenly been lifted.

"That," he said, still smiling, "would change everything, I think."

"Yes, I think you're right," Igneous said, patting Jonathan on the shoulder and walking onto the balcony. He placed his hands behind his back and gazed out at the lake and the ancient Aquamarinian runes. He breathed in that cool morning air, and he smiled. He could hear his brother getting Constance up and leading her out of the room.

That's right brother, he thought, don't you worry about me.

And as for Rose Heartington, she would be the mother of his child, even if she didn't want to be: because James Tungston's life would depend on it.

CHAPTER 31

The Woes of James

In Front of the City Decorus Regnum Corset

James was angry. No, he thought, I'm not angry. I'm furious and frustrated, not only at Rose, but the others too. Why had they let her do it? Sure, she was ready, in his opinion, but it was like walking into the mouth of a dragon and letting him eat you.

"Stupid."

He said it aloud, and while a few men were nearby, they weren't awake enough to care about what he said. He kicked the ground, but that did nothing to make him feel better or to calm his temper.

"That's not very appropriate." It was Rachel. She had willingly agreed to be Rose's double for their cause. "And what's stupid?"

"Nothing," he said hatefully, throwing a pebble to the ground. He knew that this probably wasn't an answer that would satisfy her.

"No, it's not 'nothing,' James," she said and came to stand beside him, taking his arm and looking at him. "So since it is not nothing, tell me."

While it was all an act that was used to throw off their evil neighbors, he still felt strange and uncomfortable being this close to Liam's girl. It just didn't feel right.

"Well," he said in an unsure way, looking down at her and into those warm brown eyes. Sure, he wanted to vent, but not to just anyone.

"Well?" she said, seeming to push him closer to the edge of the discussion that she knew he didn't want to enter.

"Well," he said finally, "I don't think this is a good idea."

"What do you mean by 'this,' James Tungston?" she asked politely, making him walk a little as she spoke to him.

169

"I mean you pretending to be Rose, and Rose trying to save the world on her own." He found himself looking down at the dusty path and then looking at her.

"Out of the two of us," she said, her eyes bright, and she leaned on him a little as they continued, "who do you think isn't up to the challenge?"

"Huh?"

"Well," she said softly, "you wouldn't not like it if you thought we were up to the challenge. So then the question becomes, who do you think isn't up to their end of the plan?"

"Well I think you are both capable, but..."

"There you are, then," she said, patting his arm and walking toward her tent, or rather, Rose's tent.

He hadn't even realized that they were back in the camp. Her statement was still puzzling him, and then he realized he was about to lose his chance to ask what she meant.

"I, uh," he stuttered and looked at her, "I don't understand."

He stood there now with a look of complete confusion.

"James," she said, just about to go inside to keep Damien company, "if you truly believe that we are capable of pulling this off, then she and I will be just fine."

With that she gently kissed him on the cheek.

"You needn't worry about us." And with that she turned around and went into the tent without a backward glance.

"Well," Valor said, almost sniggering and looking up at James, "she really told you."

"Oh, shut up," James grumped and walked deeper into the alley of tents. What did he care what Rachel and he had discussed?

Valor still seemed to be intent on speaking with James and was now following him through the tents.

"James," he whispered.

"Not now, Valor," James moaned, still wishing he was with Rose and the others.

"James."

"Valor, I just don't want to talk about it anymore, all right?" Here he paused to choose his next direction, not that it really mattered. The sun was up now and casting plenty of light on the scene before them. People and creatures alike were starting to stir now.

"James," Valor said quietly and sounding nervous, "it isn't about Rose."

James stopped and closed his eyes.

"It isn't?"

"No," Valor replied and began to walk over to him. "It's about the battle plan and what happens if they try to grab Rachel."

Oh, so it's about the pretend Rose, he thought.

"They won't get close enough to grab her," James said, now striding in step with Valor and heading to the front line, where men were waiting for the impending attack. They just seemed to be ready, but they were so anxious.

"They will undoubtably try, though, because they, at the moment, believe that she is Rose Heartington."

"Why would they want to capture her, though?" James said quickly as they strode behind the men sitting and waiting. He couldn't believe how calm they all were, for the most part.

"Wouldn't they just want to dispose of her, along with all of us?" James asked and looked over at Valor.

"Now that she has openly accepted her family history, and ultimately the throne, they will want her to be on their side," Valor whispered. He chanced giving James a quick glance before looking forward again.

"Igneous must know that she wouldn't join him willingly."

"Perhaps that won't matter to him," Valor replied and continued, "After all, very little does, except complete and absolute power."

"Yah." James nodded, sighing and looking at Valor with knowing eyes.

After this conversation James found he didn't want to speak to too many more individuals, animal and human alike. He spent most of the rest of the day walking around and continuously checking their precautionary defenses.

He skipped breakfast but decided eating something at the midday meal would be beneficiary. After making the decision, he swallowed a few mouthfuls of food and remembered why he had skipped the meal that came previous to this. His stomach was so tight and squirming with worry that the food made him feel as though being sick would be inevitable.

The afternoon passed in a similar form as the morning, with tensions high and many people starting to shift uncomfortably.

He walked by the front line again with a few nods to the men, women, and creatures that looked up at him. Nods of reassurance that the battle was coming, for those who felt that the battle wouldn't start soon enough. Nods of comfort to those who feared the battle itself.

Deciding that sitting would be a good idea, he found a patch of grass near Valor and leaned against him.

He sighed as he watched the sun begin to set. He knew that Rose and her party would be getting ready for their assault soon. He also knew that they were about to attempt to infiltrate the kingdom's most well-guarded building, Heartington Castle.

"Do you think they forgot we were out here?" Valor asked, half amused.

"No," James replied, "I think they want us to be off guard before…"

But his train of thought was interrupted by a high-pitched whistling sound: cannon fire.

"Everyone to your stations!" Evan ordered as several cannonballs struck tents, sending their occupants screaming.

"Come on, Valor!" he said with a loud groan and reached for his sword as the men and women in front mounted their horses, hippogriffs, griffins, or winged horses. If without a rideable, four-legged animal, they were on foot, with bows and arrows or swords and shields.

"Get up, James!" Valor whinnied loudly over the multitude of voices and sounds.

James pulled himself up and saw Topaz standing with Thomas on her shoulder just to his right. A little ways past her, Evan was on a normal horse, with Allegiance standing in a crouch just to his left. Liam too was just a few yards to his left; Enigma was poised to take down the lot of them.

"James!"

It was Pricilla and Marina Griffen, and with them their spaniels, Comis and Aurora, the latter of which was a huge contrast to Comis's crimson by being black and gold.

"Yes!" he hollered over the noise.

"Rachel is safe way back, as if we were protecting Rose!" Marina said.

"I will be returning to her, but Marina wishes to fight with all of you!" Pricilla said, choking on her own words, which were filled with emotion.

A roar came from across the way, and winged creatures of all sorts took flight as others charged.

"Very well, but hurry," he said and pulled on Valor's reigns very slightly and began to move.

"*Charge!*" Evan bellowed over the explosive sounds of stampeding men.

Battle cries could be heard on both ends of the line, and winged creatures took flight to meet those of the other side that were in the air.

"Argh!" James cringed as an arrow grazed his left arm just as he was about to reach the middle of the field.

"OK up there?" Valor said, almost inaudible in the clashes of weapons and people that were happening all around them.

"Fine!" he said, "Keep going!"

They finally reached the army before them. James drew his sword and began to fight for his life, his beliefs, and to reach the castle before Rose reached Igneous.

CHAPTER 32

The Door

Outside of the Door to the Trasicore Breeding Center

"Deep breaths, Rose," she told herself as the end of the day drew near. They had sat here for a whole twenty-four hours, or whatever it was here, she thought, waiting for the sounds of battle to erupt on the front side of the castle. The suspense was killing her, and the longer she had to wait, the harder it was to keep her nerve.

"They are whispering behind us," Nightsky said softly to Rose from her right. She was lying down with her head curled around to face Rose, her wings folded and armor on.

"That's OK," Rose said and picked at a plant that was in front of her on the ground.

She was sitting on the cold earth and had her back against a tree. The door could barely be seen through the trees before her, but she didn't need to see it to know that it was there.

The door and everything behind it loomed over her like a cloud that just wouldn't stop dropping rain. There was so much riding on her team's success. But the task would be far from easy. The door led to an enclosure filled with creatures who preferred a human for food and needed one for reproduction. If they all survived the run through the enclosure, then there was the castle itself.

The castle was huge, or at least to Rose it was, and she had to search through and find one man in it. That man was Igneous Stipes, and he was by far the most dangerous person that she had heard of. He was said to be cunning and exceptionally good at getting what he wanted, by force or otherwise. Most people wanted to avoid him, but they were setting out to find and stop this man.

"Rose." It was Aphra, and she was on her hands and knees, coming over to her.

"Yes?" Rose whispered back and turned to see that Siren was coming over as well.

"We were wondering if it would be best to move back if no fighting starts tonight?"

"Um…"

Rose was going to answer the thought, but a dull roar reached her ears.

"Rose!" hissed an excited Orpheus, "They are fighting!"

"It's time, then," Rose said, standing up slowly, not wanting to make too much noise. If they were too loud and got caught, this would all be over very quickly.

"Do you suppose it is locked?" Courage asked, practically blending into the darkness with his black exterior.

"No," Nightsky replied quickly but in a whisper, "Rachel said it wasn't ever locked because no one ever made it out."

"Besides, there is a rock at the base we press to open it," Rose whispered and found herself focusing exactly on which rock Rachel said it was. It should be right at the foot of the door and exactly where the door opens.

"And we want to go in?" Devin said, pulling out his sword. He sounded as though the idea was somewhere in between ludicrous and funny.

"Crazy, huh?" Don said, a shadow of a grin on his face.

There were only a few others with them because too large a party would draw attention. They had volunteered because they felt that they were going to be part of the most important fight of the battle. They were also, for the most part, very young and slightly less experienced. Altogether they were a party of twelve people and ten animals. Two of the volunteers hadn't even gone into the Forest of Promise to find their animal yet.

"Are we ready?" Vengeance said humorously. Apparently she thought all of this was funny. It had been clear since the meeting in the tent that she neither trusted Rose nor wanted to follow her.

Were they ready? The answer was no, but the time was now.

"On three," Rose said, holding up one hand.

"One," she mouthed, raising her pointer finger.

"Two." She raised her middle finger to join the other.

"Three."

They ran to the door, crossing the small gap between the woods and the door that was covered in short grass. Rose, reaching it first, opened it with the stone and allowed the others to go inside before following with Nightsky. Once they were all in, the door closed with an unnerving thud.

She couldn't believe the sheer size of the place. It had clearly been magically enhanced, and the light was artificial. It was a frightful place, and she couldn't wait to be out of it.

"OK," she breathed, "the other door is straight ahead from here, so everyone meet me on the other side."

Nods could be seen in the artificial light, and they all disappeared to find the door. People and animals were doing as they discussed and heading in the door's direction but taking different paths to get there. Rose and Nightsky followed, moving swiftly and silently.

The enclosure was mostly dark, with pockets of magical, artificial light. The ground was mounded and far from flat, making running on it more than challenging. Not only was the ground uneven, but boulders and rocks were strewn everywhere. The trees were massive and unearthly, looking as if magic had not only grown them but fed them. It was an overall eerie place, where the greenish lights made one feel something was about to happen.

"Ahhh!"

The scream came from her right, and without thinking she shifted her direction slightly.

"Rose!" Nightsky called after her, moving quickly to catch up.

Rose ran this way and that, dodging bushes, trees, and other obstacles before she got to the source of the scream. There, before her very eyes, was a twelve-foot trasicore, and it was holding Devin.

The creature let out its horrible roar and tightened its clawed grip around Devin's waist and legs.

"Help me!" he screamed and tried to get at his sword. The creature would have none of it, however, and switched limbs, going from using its left clawed limb to its right tentacle.

Rose pulled her sword to stab the trasicore but was lifted off her feet by something.

Upside down she saw another, smaller one now had her by the ankle and had brought her level with its face. The creature's breath was putrid, and its fangs an off yellow gray. It was just at that moment that she heard a loud crunching noise behind her that meant that Devin was no more. There was even a satisfied sort of growl after the crunching stopped.

"Argh!" she cried as she sent her sword right through the creature's head, between both sets of eyes. It dropped her and fell to the ground, and it continued to make a strange gurgling sound. She quickly righted herself, scrambling to get to her feet and searching for Nightsky.

"Nightsky!" Rose called and turned around to see her stabbing the twelve-foot creature repeatedly, though the first few times would have done it.

"You," she said, taking pauses between stabs, "evil—son—of—a—bitch!"

She stopped, out of breath and swaying a little. Apparently she was dizzy from stabbing the creature so violently. After taking a moment to steady herself, she stood upright and looked at Rose. She was so upset that it took her a moment to find her composure.

"Where's Orpheus?" Rose said, looking around, searching for the white lizard that usually stood out in every scenario he was in.

"He is there." Nightsky swallowed and looked in the direction of the trampled path that the trasicore had made. Bushes and trees had been pushed aside to make room for the trasicore's direct route to his easy meal.

Looking among the destruction, she saw something white and broken. Orpheus was flattened and centered in a dusty footprint left by the creature that had devoured his friend and companion. It was clear to Rose that Orpheus had tried to intervene and save his friend, but size made a difference in this fight and Orpheus had lost.

"He didn't stand a chance," Nightsky whinnied and stamped her hooves.

"I know, Nightsky," Rose said dolefully. "I know."

Rose took another quick look around and noted that she was out of breath from the fighting. This was not going to be easy, as they had already lost two, and that was two too many.

"We need to move before more of those things smell the blood," Nightsky said, looking around nervously.

"Yah," Rose breathed and started to look around and regain focus in the process. Seeing a path that must have been made by repetitive movement gave Rose an idea.

"What do you want to bet that following that path will lead up to the door to the castle?" Rose said, starting to move with Nightsky right behind her.

"Could be," Nightsky replied as she ran to keep up with Rose.

The path was dusty and smooth, very different from the rest of the terrain. Rose could only hope that the path led to where she thought, because they were trekking farther and farther into the enclosure with every step.

She was just starting to worry that she had made a poor choice when she came upon the clearing that Rachel had described and saw an ancient-looking wood door with the same copper finishing.

"Nightsky," she breathed heavily, pointing at the door as she continued to run.

In reaching the door, she stopped and placed a hand to her chest, still breathing hard. It wasn't long before others from their party arrived, and it soon became clear that they had lost the better half of their party. Don and Vengeance came trudging through the same area that Rose had, and Courage was only seconds behind them. Nightmare flew to the ground and seemed to have been monitoring the situation from above and explained that most of the rest of their party had become a late-night meal for the trasicores.

"Not only have they eaten, but somehow the door opened in the back, and now they are free and out in the world," Nightmare said and looked as though she might like to rip someone's throat out.

"Oh great," Nightsky glowered, "now we have to worry about more of them out there."

It was as the group was freaking out about the loose creatures that Siren, Aphra's sapphire fox, came tottering into the clearing.

"Siren," Rose started to ask, concerned and fearing the worst, "where's Aphra?"

"I'm here." Rose had to turn around in a half circle to see Aphra leaning on the door and bleeding from her right leg very badly.

"I was attacked by a small one," she said in explanation, looking up at the horrified group.

"If Siren hadn't run in front of it and offered a distraction..." She sighed and looked at the fox gratefully, "I would not have been able to get away."

"How are we going to move around with her like that?" Vengeance hissed angrily and reaffirming Rose's deep dislike of her.

"She'll be all right," Don said firmly, looking at Vengeance with a questioning look. "I'll look after her."

Rose nodded and looked at the few left to take the castle. It wasn't looking good, but it was now or never, and she looked at Nightsky. She read the message loud and clear.

"Ready?" Nightsky asked them all, her horn starting to glow.

There were several slight nods around the group and, with Rose's nod giving the go-ahead, Nightsky turned back toward the door.

There was a sudden flash of brilliant light that emanated from her horn, followed by the soft click of a door unlocking. There was a creak, and the door lay open before them.

Rose held her breath, waiting to see if they would be met with resistance. No one came.

"Go!" Rose whispered urgently and quickly. They all piled through.

The room was just as Rachel described it. A wall that was a window. A hallway that led right from the door to a prison keep and a second hallway running parallel to the glass wall. The second hallway started with four intricate pillars that led to an archway, signifying the entrance.

"All right," Rose said softly and looked around, "let's split up as soon as we reach the surface."

"One group to take the king and the other to let our army into the castle and city?" Vengeance said, taking over and annoying Nightsky enough for her to snort in irritation.

"Right," Rose whispered and was about to break off when a very unwelcome sight appeared in the corner of her eyes.

Soldiers that outnumbered them three to one came charging in. It was as if they had known that they would be there.

Crap, Rose thought and prepared herself for the fight that was going to happen. But before she could get herself ready, Vengeance made her move.

"Charge!" she screamed, cutting down two men in one blow and engaging a third. Nightmare soon joined her, taking on several animals that belonged to the soldiers.

Having no other choice, Rose, too, engaged a foe and cut him across the back, kicking him out of the way.

"Rose, behind you!" came a frantic Courage, who was dealing with a gray wolf attempting to bite his ankles.

Rose turned and took in a sharp breath as a man came running toward her, sword raised. Rose tried to ready herself when in mid-run, he suddenly made a noise that sounded like the air had been sucked out of him. Rose watched as he fell to the ground, his eyes wide and face blank.

Where he had been standing was Nightsky's horn, horizontal to the floor and in a stabbing position. She brought her head upright and composed herself as Rose mouthed, "Thank you." Nightsky nodded and, after kicking another guard, joined Rose by the first of the pillars.

"Go!" someone called from inside the fray, and Rose craned her neck to see who it was.

"Just go, Rose!" It was Don. He and Vengeance were in the thick of it, with Courage and Nightmare doing their best to keep the other animals away from their humans. Aphra was trying her best to lend a hand in the battle, and Siren was nipping and scratching wherever she could.

Rose looked on the scene, with Nightsky waiting impatiently for her to go. Rose wanted to help but wasn't sure how; she couldn't just leave them, could she? Vengeance broke free with Nightmare and was running.

"*Go!*" Don cried again, and Rose nodded.

She turned and ran through the archway and down the hall with Nightsky, Vengeance and Nightmare only steps behind her.

CHAPTER 33

Exotius Obscurum

In the City Decorus Regnum Corset

*S*ince the battle had begun, night had fallen, and so had many a brave man, woman, and animal. The battle was in full rage at this point, and there were no clear lines anymore. The only thing that was clear was the fact that the army of RTET was gaining ground and nearing the city's walls.

James and Valor were in the thick of it, and they were finally in sight of the city's gates. James had deserted his saddle and was now on foot with most of the others, as he had made a prime target on top of Valor. The men he had been fighting were tough and didn't give up easily. Very few men gave in to defeat, and most died first before withdrawing. Neither side wanted to give in to the other.

"They're retreating!" came the cry of a fellow member of his army, and some of the others cheered. James, however, didn't think that it could possibly be that easy: not with Igneous and Exotius.

"Keep focused, everyone!" He heard Evan call firmly from somewhere in the distance. James looked around to find his leader and caught a glimpse of him about fifty yards in front of him. Allegiance was only feet away from Evan and lashed out at a soldier charging and roared.

James and the rest of the army of RTET pushed forward, glad to gain new ground without having to fight tooth and nail for it. But it soon became clear that they weren't going to gain the next bit of ground so easily.

After running most of the distance between their army and the king's, they saw that the king's army had received reinforcements. The gates had opened, and men were now lining up to charge the enemy with renewed fury, and to make matters worse, they had some new creatures on their side.

It seemed that Rachel's story about the king breeding trasicores was true, because there stood five of them, and they were the largest that James had ever seen or even heard of. They were pushing twenty feet tall, and they had limbs that were as long as a man is tall. Horror was all James felt at the sight of them. How was the army supposed to beat that?

"Oh, man." James swallowed and stopped with the rest of the army.

"Evan!" Topaz called from somewhere on James's right, "How do we get past that!?"

"By praying we are the lucky ones," Valor whispered in James's ear. He had found his way next to him and was limping, having been injured by a stray arrow that had grazed his right foreleg.

"Everyone!" Evan hollered, and he now had the whole army's attention.

"You pledged to do all that was necessary to bring this regime to its knees. You said that you would fight, even if you only had one leg to stand on and held a sword in your only remaining arm to finish this tyrant of a king."

He paused, turning in his saddle to survey them and their tired, dirty faces. He had them all waiting with bated breath to hear what he had to say.

"Don't quit now," he said with an urgency that made James want to win even more. "Not now, when we are so close. So close to victory. So close to freedom."

He rode slightly forward and turned his horse to face them all. He too looked battle tired and seemed to want to rest. But it was his face that told a different story. His face said that he still had a lot of fight in him yet.

"They," he said, looking at them and pointing at the army behind him, "hide like cowards behind those horrifying beasts because they know they are beaten by purpose. By pride. By honor. That we will not stop until justice prevails and peace reigns throughout."

He watched them all hold their breath.

"My friends," he breathed and readied himself, "you are my family, and I would be willing to die alongside you. I am honored to be the one leading you out of the time of darkness and into a future of warmth and light."

There was not a pair of eyes that were not upon him. There was not a sound that could be heard.

"So let us end this," he said in a low growl. "Let us cut off the head of tyranny and hold it high to the dawn of freedom!"

There was a huge cry of approval from the army behind him. An army that, only moments ago, was filled with defeat and fear. But now they held their swords high and raised their bows and cheered on their leader, ready for the next stint of fighting. And looking toward the gates as if freedom emanated from the city beyond them.

"To victory!" Evan cried, charging forward at the center trasicore, Allegiance was running in his wake, ready to take down the creature single-handedly.

There was a great roar as the army of RTET charged forward behind him and clashed once more with the king's army of annihilation. James was one of the first to reach the army after Evan, and he sank his sword into the first soldier he encountered. Valor was right behind him, trampling many under his hooves and causing some to move out of his way to save themselves.

But the trasicores had since been released, and many a person and creature were now being crushed or swallowed by the beasts. Their limbs were flailing, and even when they became unbalanced they did damage, killing or injuring any who came near them.

Just then a horrifying scream came from his right, and he watched with utter terror as a trasicore sank its fangs into his sister, Topaz, piercing her chest and stomach in one go. It opened its mouth and wrapped its tongue around the wound, sucking horribly.

"Nooo!" he screamed in rage and redirected his attention on the creature, jumping onto Valor and racing forward. His sword found many a soldier as they galloped in Topaz's direction, Valor crushing all who were unfortunate enough to end up beneath him. But James's lust for blood existed for no man at this point; it was only there for that foul creature.

"Thomas, no!" Valor whinnied as the raven tried frantically to cause the creature to release her.

But the trasicore would not be distracted from a meal it had and swatted Thomas without a care. It was about to step on him just at James drove his sword into its right front leg.

The creature let out a terrifying sound and began thrashing as it limped on the rest of its five legs. Trying to keep its balance, it decided to drop Topaz and defend itself.

"Valor, get Topaz!" he cried, jumping off and preparing to fight.

The trasicore raised a clawed arm and swung. James was ready and cut the limb off with one stroke. The blow from him was directly followed by a blow from the creature's tentacle, sending him flying. He rolled over and grabbed his sword just in time to avoid being stepped upon.

"Argh!"

He cried, swinging his sword and hitting it across its back, causing it to release another cry.

"Take that, you—"

His sentence was interrupted by its tongue wrapping around his waist and lifting him up over fourteen feet and banging him against the wall. He was dazed, and it took him a moment to refocus. The creature had dropped him just to pick him back up and bring him up to his razor-sharp teeth.

Using up a massive amount of effort, he swung his sword and cut off the creature's tongue. The creature started to writhe, and James landed hard at the creature's feet.

"James!"

It was Valor, but he needed to wait until James was finished with this creature from hell. With an effort that was second only to his last stand, he drove his sword into the monster's chest and wrenched it out as it fell.

He was breathing heavily and continued to glare at the dead or dying creature.

"Well, I must say I am impressed."

James felt the hair on the back of his neck stand up. He quickly swung around and found himself face to face with Igneous Stipes's right hand man, Exotius Obscurum.

"Yah, well…" James said, not quite knowing how to finish his sentence.

"However," Exotius said, drawing his own sword, Wildfire readying himself behind him, "Your father was once a great fighter, and look how he turned out."

Oh, that does it, James thought, and letting out a cry of absolute rage, he ran, sword raised, at his father's murderer.

Wildfire was now met with opposition from Valor, who was now biting, pushing, and kicking to keep him from getting to James. And Wildfire was doing the same.

The fight between the animals was nothing compared to that of their human partners. James and Exotius were trading blows with such ferocity that their arms shook and their bones rattled. Exotius was quite strong and was throwing blows at James that made James wonder if this fight was going to end in his favor.

He threw another swing at Exotius, but this time when their swords met, Exotius grabbed his arm, held it fast, and said,

"You can't win." He smiled and continued, "And when you're dead, I'm going to kill your friends, the rest of your family, and then I'm going to give your girlfriend to the king on a silver platter."

He threw James against the wall, and James rolled out of the way just as Exotius took a swing.

"Yah," James said, and their swords met a few more times before he punched Exotius in the mouth, sending him backward this time. "Well, when you're dead, I'm going to feed *you* to the first animal that'll have you!"

Exotius grinned evilly. Apparently he liked that James still had some spirit in him to keep the fight interesting. He then took up his sword again and resumed their fight, taking a swing at James before running through the gates. James ran after him, determined to take him down.

James was now running past the rest of Igneous's army as it filtered through the gate and was heading toward the castle and after Exotius. He could see him heading for the castle's gate, and James redoubled his efforts to reach him, running right through the fountain and not slowing. He was using every ounce of speed he had so as to reach him.

"What's the matter, Exotius? You afraid to fight me?" James said, stopping just as Exotius reached the castle's drawbridge. "Afraid you'll lose?"

Exotius stopped just short of the bridge and turned around. That's done it, James thought. Exotius's sense of pride had prevented him from continuing; it was known throughout the kingdom, and James had just attacked it.

"Araagh!!" Exotius cried, his eyes red as blood now and faster with his sword than ever before. He came at James, swinging left, then right, then left again. Each swing more brutal than the last, and James was doing all he could to keep up with him. But in Exotius's haste to win, he lost his balance, and James seized his chance. He swung at Exotius's chest and grazed it, drawing blood.

This, however, only enraged him further, and he began fighting James with renewed rage, knocking him to the ground and cutting him across the chest.

"I hope, James Tungston," Exotius said smiling, placing one foot on James's chest to hold him to the ground, "that you enjoyed insulting me. Because that insult is going to be your last."

James watched as Exotius, with his eyes blazing, brought his sword up for the kill.

"Say hi to your father for me."

Then, as he was about to bring his sword crashing down, another blade went and pierced him through the chest.

The look on Exotius Obscurum's face was one of pure shock and disbelief, and he stood there, swaying a moment. James could see what was going to come next and rolled out of the way as he fell flat on his face, with the sword still in him.

James looked up and saw that Rachel MacNeil now stood where Exotius once had. She held out a hand in an offer to help James to his feet.

"That," she said, wrenching the sword out of Exotius and glaring at his dead form, "is for Danny and Tormen."

"Thank you," James whispered, patting her arm and breathing heavily.

"No need to thank me," she said, wiping a tear from her eye. "You would do the same for me."

James nodded.

"Of course we would," came the voice of Valor.

James turned and saw his horse limping in his direction. James also noticed that the fight had now entered the city, and people were getting closer to the castle.

"Where's Wildfire?" James asked, filled with curiosity.

"Oh, him," Valor said with an air of something that needn't be discussed, "he fell into a trasicore's dead, open mouth and impaled himself on its teeth."

"Eeee," Rachel's cat, Damien, had arrived and shivered at the thought, "that must have hurt."

"Ah, well," Valor said breezily, "that's the way life goes."

James suddenly realized how close he was to the castle, and in that case, Rose. He let out an involuntary groan and looked at the building.

"James," Rachel said softly, and they watched as the space remaining between them and the castle filled with other groups of fighters. "Go."

"Go?" he said absentmindedly.

She smiled and looked up at the castle.

"Go and help her."

"I am supposed to keep you safe," James said, looking at her and smiling a small smile before looking at the castle again.

"I'll keep her safe, kid."

It was Liam, and it felt as though he had appeared out of nowhere.

"Don't worry," Enigma growled, walking right behind Liam, "we won't let a thing happen to her."

Damien hopped onto Enigma's back and curled up.

"We'll make sure that every soldier from here to Lake Veteris Spiritus falls before she does," Liam said, smiling.

"Go, James." She whispered in his ear and kissed his cheek, "Help the one you love."

"I'll see you when it's over?" James said in more of a question to Liam.

"'Course, kid," Liam said firmly, readying his sword as soldiers approached, "I wouldn't want to miss your wedding."

James nodded and turned to Valor, who was waiting for him. James climbed up on him, ready for the next fight. James took a final look at the four of them and watched them fight with renewed force as they took on a new group of soldiers.

James and Valor then turned and started toward the castle. They ran past groups of fighters, but James knew he needed to focus on the fight he was most likely to have next. They finally crossed the drawbridge and were crossing the courtyard, and James knew that the next villain he met would be far worse than the last.

CHAPTER 34

The Garden

ose and Vengeance had just reached the top of the staircase that led back into the courtyard and away from the trasicore enclosure and the soldiers.

"How do we get out?" Nightmare crowed, ruffling her wings.

"Like this!" Vengeance cried, and using the tip of the blade of her sword, she pushed the tip of it into a notch right in the middle of the ceiling and next to the door's frame.

The door immediately opened, and Vengeance ran through, Nightmare following her with assurance.

"How did she know what to do?" Rose asked Nightsky and turned to look at her. Nightsky looked dumbstruck and stared blankly at her and then after the other two.

"I know that she's close to Rachel, but Rachel only told me about that," Rose said and had an uneasy feeling as she watched Vengeance cut down the two guards that were posted at the door leading into the castle.

"Come on!" Nightmare hissed at the two of them as Vengeance entered the castle.

Rose nodded and ran from the stable across the courtyard, and after checking that the coast was still clear, nodded to Nightsky. Nightsky trotted across, her hooves causing echoes across the courtyard. Once at the door, Rose looked around and across the yard; there was most certainly no going back from here.

They had finally made it to the castle, Rose thought as she ran down the hallway and saw the cabinet that Rachel had described.

Suddenly there was some crazed whinnying and cries of rage from a group of soldiers. Infestus was galloping toward them from the other end of the hallway, with soldiers right behind him.

"I don't think we invited them to our party," Nightmare said, stretching out her claws and swiping at the first soldier she saw.

"Let's throw them out, then," Nightsky said, spearing another soldier with her horn.

Rose and Vengeance worked hard to get through the group. Rose injured two men and ducked a well-placed blow from another. Vengeance was fending off Infestus and attempting to kill him, by the looks of it. The horse made a mad effort to get to Rose and bit the upper part of Vengeance's arm.

"Ahh!" Vengeance let out an involuntary cry.

"Vengeance!" Nightmare said, impaling and tossing two guards, leaving only one and Infestus.

"Take that," Nightsky growled and kicked the guard in the head, knocking him to the ground and watching as he let out a gargling sound.

"She's mine!" Infestus said in a deep undertone and charged at Vengeance, attempting to trample her and giving her the opportunity she needed.

Vengeance drove her sword right through the horse's chest, being knocked down in the process. Infestus fell to the ground and moved no more.

"Take that, you—" but Nightmare's next word was quite vulgar, and Rose decided to drown it out.

"How's your arm?" Rose asked, looking concerned and walking over to her and looking at her arm.

"Sore, but I'll live," she groaned and pulled her arm out of Rose's reach so she couldn't see it.

She is just a huge pain, Rose thought, and she isn't about to follow me anywhere. Her intention is to lead.

"He was a huge pain in the you-know-where for sure," Nightmare said as they finally stood in front of the cabinet at the end of the hallway.

"I think," Vengeance said, breathing hard and looking at Rose in a strange way, "now would be a good time to split up."

"It will be easier for us to conquer the two brothers by dividing," Nightmare muttered distractedly as she looked down the right side of the hallway.

"OK," Rose breathed.

Then all four of them began to break off into different directions and fulfill their different tasks.

Nightsky, Rose, and Vengeance went left, while Nightmare went right. Nightmare was going to try to locate the throne room and see what she could find there. The other three continued together in silence until Nightsky broke off down a hallway on her right. She was going down into the dungeons in order to free those who were truly innocent.

Rose and Vengeance continued down the hallway, and they walked in silence until they reached the entrance hall and saw the stairs leading up.

"Look."

Rose's sudden aggression had captured Vengeance's attention.

"I don't know what your issue is with me, but drop it."

Vengeance looked Rose up and down as her eyebrows went up.

"Well," she said in disbelief, "you suddenly became quite aggressive and accusatory."

"I don't even think that you're from around here."

Vengeance had a strange look in her eyes and smiled.

"Maybe I am," she said and walked over to Rose and continued to look at her, "maybe I'm not. But that shouldn't matter as, at the moment, I'm on your side."

"'At the moment' doesn't sit well with me." Rose said, glaring at her.

Vengeance seemed to be thinking about something nasty, but then her face changed and became far more pleasant, as if she had just been reunited with her best friend.

"I'm sorry that you feel that way, Rose," she said earnestly, almost looking apologetic.

Rose didn't know what to say and looked at the woman before her with a wary expression. She knew that this woman couldn't be trusted, but to trust her now was far from being an option; it was a necessity. She decided to make amends for now and bring this back up later.

"Fine," Rose said coolly, "let's just get this over with."

"Fine," she said slyly, heading for the stairs.

Rose and Vengeance walked up the first flight of stairs together. In reaching the landing, Vengeance broke off and headed toward Jonathan's end of the castle, not even giving Rose a backward glance. Rose shook her head and started up the next flight of stairs. This flight would lead her to the king's quarters and hopefully, yet terribly, him.

It's so quiet up here, Rose thought as she reached the landing and looked down the hallway. Maybe, she thought, they fled from here after the others breached the city walls. Yah, she thought, smiling weakly, that'll be the day.

The hallway seemed so long to her, but that was more nerves than actuality. There were several doors, and each could lead to the room she wanted. From what she had been told, there was a library at the very end of the hall and then a study that was next to it. Wait, she thought, what side was the study on?

If someone were to come by now, they would be met by a very strange sight. She was covered in sweat and blood, both human and animal alike. She was just standing there, as still as can be, and looking as though she had been frozen in time.

Shaking her head, she began to take the first of many careful steps forward. She held her sword loosely but was ready to use it if she had to. That day she even took a secondary weapon with her by using a dagger to hold up her hair.

After some deductive reasoning, she decided to take the first door on her left. It seemed to be the best choice, and in coming beside it, she leaned against the wall. She took a deep breath as if to prepare for going underwater. She grasped the door handle, opened the door, and dashed in.

The room, however elegant, was empty. But it was clearly the king's room, for the room could belong to no other. A huge portrait of the king stood just past the fireplace on her left-hand side and stood almost seven feet tall. In it, he was holding both arms across his chest, and a tree surrounded by bushes was just to his right. He was dressed in gray armor, and one hand could be seen resting on the pommel of his sword. His expression was rather smug.

"Well," she whispered aloud, "he thinks rather highly of himself, doesn't he?"

She walked over to it, marveling at its sheer size. He wasn't, in her opinion, that far from being good looking, but the evil in his eyes, which spread across face, was not. This took away all hope of anyone taking any notice of his nicer features.

Brr, she thought as a cool breeze ran across her. That's weird, she thought, Despite the warm fire next to this spot, there is cold air near the painting. She turned to see if the balcony doors were open; they weren't.

"I wonder," she whispered and placed her hand near the frame. Cold air was flowing from behind it.

Well, she thought, looking around for something that would open it. After all, in Earth movies, there was always a knob or button or book that opened the secret door; why wouldn't that work for him? Taking a step closer to it, after looking all around it, she was looking to see if she could pry it open. Then she tripped over a loose stone in the floor and lost her balance and fell through the doorway and almost down some stairs before she stopped herself.

"Ow," she groaned and winced as she stood up. She had a few cuts on her arms from going straight through the wooden back of the frame. But she was more concerned by the semi-dark nature of the stairwell that lay before her.

At that very thought, the tiara on her head began to glow again, illuminating the space and renewing her confidence as she started down the stairs. Rose had nearly forgotten she had been wearing the tiara, because the original plan had been for Rachel to wear it. Then, as she had been about to give it to Rachel, a rather wealthy family offered a similar-looking headdress of roughly the same size and color for Rachel to wear. This left the original in Rose's possession and on her head.

Farther on, the staircase was lined with torches, and it seemed as though they had been lit recently. Each step took her farther down the side of the castle, then the air got damp and cool, which told her that she was belowground. She even smelled fresh earth, which she found very strange.

She couldn't help thinking that this trip down these stairs was going to take her a lifetime, and as she walked, she could feel her heart pounding in her ears. Each throb of her heart matched the step she took the farther down she went. Then she didn't see any more stairs.

At last, she thought as she reached the bottom and was faced with yet another door. This was doing nothing for her anxieties and her mounting fears.

Behind that door could be something truly terrifying, or worse: Igneous himself. It could be a trap. Yet, she thought, no going back, and not going in would be backing out on my own plan.

She breathed deeply and looked at the plainest door she had seen since she had been on this planet. It was made out of wood, and it wasn't anything special. It wasn't as mysterious as the door to this world. Nor did it have the ingenuity of the bed frame door. This door wasn't even as creative as the door she had fallen through to get to this door. She started toward it and reached out her hand.

But before she could open it, it swung open, like the automatic ones back on Earth. There were no such doors here, though, she thought, Must be magic.

Slowly and cautiously, she stepped through the door. The room smelled of fresh earth, and the ground was grass, and cut through it was a single path made of some dirt and gravel. It was filled with plants of about the same size, and they were all roughly the same build. Each plant was arranged in a pattern that followed the single path, which was leading to the center of the room.

The room itself was a rough oval shape, and the walls weren't covered in stone, like the rest of the building, but vines that held the earth in place. There were four large crystalline objects that lined the walls and emitted a strange yet pure white light.

The center of the room was marked by a single large rock, oddly shaped but with a smooth top, as if someone had sat there constantly. The rock was not huge by any stretch of the imagination, but in thinking about the wear on it, she definitely felt a grown man could easily sit there.

There was a sudden but soft thud, and she jumped slightly. The door had closed behind her, and with a quick look around, she could tell that she was still alone. Curiosity was starting to take hold of her now and was urging her to continue forward.

She loved all plants and had learned about quite a few of them through her father and his flower shop. Her favorite were flowering plants, but those that didn't flower were just as interesting.

She began to venture into the room and toward the center. She wanted to get a closer look at the plant that was set right in front of the rock. While the light from the crystals was better than nothing, the brilliant green light her headdress emitted allowed her to be able to see the whole room.

I must be under a garden, she thought, still admiring all the roots that followed the ceiling and walls. The smell of the fresh earth brought back wonderful memories of her father and their garden.

"Don't crowd them," he told her, smiling. "They need their space, too, you know."

"Yay," she said, smiling and looking at the evenly spaced plants around her. They needed their space too, she thought. She was only a few steps away from the bush now and was more sure of herself than she had been in the whole time she had been here.

Once she reached the plant, she stopped admiring the simplicity of it all. Here was a room filled with plants, filled with life, and yet just above them death was in abundance. Yet this plant somehow seemed very important. She crouched down to examine it. As she did so, she saw immediately and unquestionably what this plant was.

This plant, in fact all of these plants, were rose bushes. She could tell by the thorny stems and vines as well as the shape of the leaves.

"They must all be rose bushes," she breathed softly and stood up, examining the room before looking down at the bush again.

She just couldn't understand why it would have no flowers, since it seemed to be a relatively healthy plant. She knelt down and looked sadly at a plant that she believed to be on its way out. She reached out a hand and gently caressed one of the leaves.

Then she felt a soft breeze and stood up to survey the room. Every plant began to move and rustle its leaves. Stems started to grow, and the kind of process that usually took days happened in an instant. Soon she saw some bushes start to climb trellises as buds grew on their stems, while others grew buds on stems of stationary bushes. Soon she was surrounded by rosebuds, hundreds of them, and one by one they began to open.

What she saw took her breath away. There were roses of sapphire and of opal. Roses of red rubies and pure white pearls. One rose bush had blooms of breathtaking topaz. There were bushes of aquamarine, jade, and diamond. Some held many tourmalines, each bloom more beautiful than the next. While still others sported blooms of onyx, peridot, and garnet.

Then the last of the buds opened into brilliant and breathtaking emeralds. The emerald roses formed on the bush right in front of her.

She couldn't believe her eyes. She was now surrounded by hundreds of priceless gems and jewels. These bushes had been a part of the story James had told her.

"James *was* telling the truth," Rose whispered in awe.

"And apparently didn't teach you a thing."

CHAPTER 35

The King

The Bejeweled Garden

R ose swung around and found herself face to race with the life-size version of the individual in the painting up the stairs. The only thing was, he didn't have any of the painting's charm. The real Igneous Stipes was far more intimidating in person than she would have thought, and he was blocking her exit.

"I'm not sure what you mean by that," Rose said and was glad to hear the steadiness in her voice, because the rest of her was shaking.

"No?" he said, smiling and looking her up and down.

"No," she retorted and glared back.

"Well let me explain myself, then." With those words he took a few careful steps toward her. She in turn took a step back.

"He let you wander into this castle all on your own. Knowing full well who and what resided here." He continued to smile and walk toward her, "And yet he still let you come and allowed you to think you could just walk around in here."

"See, you are wrong there," Rose said, retreating one more step as he continued to advance. "He told me that I should allow him to come, but I told him no. That in order to maintain the illusion that I was across the way, he had to be there and not with me."

Igneous took two more steps and raised his eyebrows at her as he did so; she couldn't back up any further. He was now in the center of the circle with her, and only a few feet separated them.

"Well," he whispered, grinning evilly and looking at her, "I guess I was underestimating him then, wasn't I? And…"

He paused and took a few more steps, leaving only the rock between them, and Rose took a step back and put the rock and the emerald rose bush between them.

"...wrong about you."

"Really?" Rose breathed and leaned back a little, keeping the distance and hoping that talking would give her a chance to conceive a plan.

"Yes," he said shortly, "really."

"In what way?"

"Well, I thought he was the fool and that you, blinded by love, were just doing what he asked you to." He paused and stepped around the rock, only leaving the bush between them. "Now I see that it is just the opposite of what I thought."

Here he drew his sword and stood very sturdily in front of her. She couldn't help but think he looked quite impressive with his sword in his hands, and that she was in for a really long fight.

"You see, I now know that *you* are the fool, and *he* is blinded by love and did as you asked."

He swung and she, barely keeping her balance, raising her own sword and blocked the blow. They then moved a quarter turn to her left, and now the door was within reach of them both.

"I'm no fool," Rose said, looking into those eyes filled with fire. "I know you killed my ancestor and that you intend to kill me."

This time Rose made a move, and he blocked, and they took a quarter turn to the right. They were back where they started, and the door was no longer an option.

"Common knowledge." He grinned. "Why don't you tell me something a little more impressive, won't you, because that wasn't."

They took a couple more swings at each other, and she was now three-quarters of the way to the left and still in a fight for the exit.

"How about this?" she said, almost getting his chest, causing him to back up slightly, and it gave her a firmer footing. "Your ultimate goal for the end of this fight is to destroy my bloodline."

"Ah," he smiled a little unnervingly and continued, "twenty-one years ago that would have been true."

This time he swung, and it was her turn to jump out of the way. She was once again blocked from the door by him.

"What's changed your mind?" she said, trying to get him off balance, but he was a superb fighter.

More clashing of the swords, and he got her just above her left shoulder.

"Arghhh!" she cried out and backed up from him but quickly regained her composure.

"Actually," he said, smiling evilly and coming quite close to her, "my plans for you have since changed. You see, you finding that tiara changes the rules."

"The rules?" she asked with difficulty as she tried to back away and still fight.

"Yes," he said and moved toward her, intensifying his level of fight, "the rules of how this game of cat versus mouse is played. Because now, in order for my rule to continue, I need an heir of royal birth."

"Sucks to be you, then," Rose said with a halfhearted smile, "because I don't know of any royalty that'll want you."

They took a couple more shots at each other, and Rose finally found herself facing the door with her back. Somehow I mustn't let him know I'm where I want to be, she thought and continued the fight.

"I don't really care if you do want me," he said and smiled at the instant reaction on her face. She clearly had given him the satisfaction of knowing she was caught by surprise.

"Excuse me?" she stuttered and could feel the blood draining from her face.

"I think you heard me."

"Yah, and I was hoping that I had heard wrong," Rose said in a high voice and started to take a step back as he advanced.

She could see where this was going, and it wasn't someplace that she wanted to go. He wasn't her type, anyway. She saw him about to swing and ducked. She swung at him and kicked out. She got him in the knee, and he stumbled back, and he seemed more than a little surprised.

She knew that this was her chance and ran toward the door; the challenge of the stairs lay ahead. She bolted across the room and through the door that opened for her and up the stairs.

With each stair her armor got heavier, and her footsteps echoed off of the walls. She could barely breathe when she reached the hole in the painting and had to quickly but carefully clamber through it.

Out of breath, she made a run for the door that led back to the hall, hoping that by getting ahead she might gain the advantage. But in her haste, she tripped over the same stone she had earlier and hit the floor hard. She swore.

She was about to get up when someone grabbed her by the hair and dragged her to her feet.

"I don't care how hard you scream or fight, sweetheart, you are going to have my kid," Igneous said with the effort of holding her in his voice.

"Over my dead body!" she cried, and holding her hands together in a fist, hit him hard in the gut.

He made some form of a grunting noise and released her. Scrambling to her feet, she ran for the door once again, but a hand caught her foot, and she met the hard floor once more.

"Oh," she groaned, dazed by the sudden impact. She rolled over, her head continuing to spin.

"You fool!" he growled, and she could just see his outline as her vision was slightly blurred, "Running isn't going to help your cause!"

She continued to moan and suddenly felt a sharp tug on her arm as he lifted her up and threw her onto the bed.

"Come now, Rose," he taunted, using magic to cut off everything but the underwear layer on her upper body and her pants, "where's your fighting spirit?"

"Right here, sire!"

She kicked him in the head as hard as she could and tried to get up off of the bed.

He recovered rather fast, however, and was now standing up with a cut over his right eye.

"Wretch!" he hollered and whacked her across the face, and she fell halfway on the bed.

He lifted her gruffly and threw her on the bed, getting on top of her.

"It's over, sweetheart," he said, holding onto her wrists and smiling down at her, "I've won. You, those people out there fighting because they think you had a chance against me. You've all lost."

"Not yet, we haven't," she said, and reaching into her hair, she pulled out the dagger and stabbed him in the arm.

He let out a yell and released her.

Realizing the mistakes of her last two attempts, she bolted fast. She then grabbed her sword and ran to the door.

"This is not good," Rose hissed as she ran down the hall and toward the stairs.

She could hear him swearing, and then there were hurried footsteps behind her that told her he was chasing her.

Oh yah, she thought, I'm in big trouble now. Nightsky, where in the hell are you?

She continued down all the stairs until she reached the entrance hall. The doors were open, and people and animals alike were now fighting in the halls. Some were even fighting on the stairs that she had just run down.

Then it struck her: Nightmare should be in the throne room. If I can get there, I'll have some help available to me, she thought and ran in the direction she believed would lead her there.

"Stop her!" The king yelled from behind her, and she knew that she needed to move faster and picked up the pace. Soldiers, however, were forced to continue their own fights, as they were having troubles of their own. She ran down one hallway and then the next until she reached what she believed to be the throne room.

"Nightmare?!" Rose called but soon saw that she was going to have to figure things out on her own.

Nightmare was fighting a snow leopard with bloodred spots, and Vengeance was fighting a man with similarities to Igneous.

"Rose!" Vengeance said in the midst of the struggle and ducking only just in time, "Rose, get out of here!"

An arm grabbed her from behind and turned her around gruffly. She had a sneaking suspicion of who it was before she saw him.

"Oh, she's not going anywhere!" Igneous breathed in her ear as he leaned in near her face.

"I haven't had my last say yet!" Rose groaned and took the heel of her boot and rammed it into his foot.

"Argh!"

Rose didn't get time to use her sword, however, because he sent her flying into a pillar.

"Aw!"

She groaned and saw in horror that he was now sending flames in her direction. I guess he's changed his mind about wanting me alive, she thought.

Well, she thought and closed her eyes as the flames drew closer, this really is the end. Her heart was breaking; she now knew that her best wasn't good enough.

Why hadn't the fire hit her yet? She opened her eyes and saw, with great relief, the form of Nightsky.

"Hang in there, Rose!"

"Nightsky," she sighed and gave her a loving look.

She watched as the fire spread over the two of them in a dome, and it was as if they had fallen into a giant ember. Nightsky continued to point her horn at the flames.

"What took you so long!" Rose hollered, finding her aggravation at last.

"I was busy!" Nightsky responded and went over to help Nightmare as Rose started to fight with Igneous, who had gone to help the other man.

"Busy with what!" she said, giving the fight her all.

"Can't you two discuss this later!" Nightmare yelled as the leopard bared her teeth and swiped at her.

"No, keep going—don't mind us," the other man yelled and almost lost his head.

She could see that Igneous was distracted by what must be his brother and his very skilled opponent.

She began to fight with every move she knew and every ounce of skill she had, and it seemed to be working. They moved away from the other two and were now in the center of the room.

He hit her hard, but she continued to fight and got his arm with her sword.

"I don't care how powerful they come," Rose said as their swords clashed and her body twisted and turned. "They, like all their predecessors that felt that they owned it all, they—will—*fall!*"

She said these last three words with blows from her sword that were powerful and that shook even his strong arms.

Then, with a tremendous effort, she knocked his sword from his hands, kicking him to the ground.

"Nope," she hissed and kicked his sword out of his reach. She then used her foot to hold his hand down and pointed her sword at his chest. The tip of it rested on top of his heart. If he has one, she thought.

"Now," she breathed, her chest heaving, oblivious to all but him, "leave my kingdom, and don't come back."

Her eyes were filled with electricity, and it was as if the ocean in them was connected to a live wire. Then, when she was sure her point had been made, she moved away from him, removing her foot from his hand.

She was just turning to the door when she heard someone shout.

"Noooo!"

She whirled around and had just enough time to see Igneous raise his sword to her just as another went straight through his heart.

CHAPTER 36

Life and Death

Heartington Castle

*I*gneous still stood before Rose, his arm raised, but shock intermixed with anger was upon his face. Whoever was behind him gave a great pull followed by a grunt, and the king fell to the floor. Once Rose's overall shock subsided, she stopped looking at the king's dead form and looked at the person who had killed him.

"James!"

Rose ran into his arms and kissed him repeatedly. He placed an arm around her and was still holding the sword in his hand.

"You complete ass, James Tungston!" she said, pulling away from him and pushing him away for a moment. "What took you so long!"

"Well, how do you like that?" He grinned, looking at Valor and then continuing, "See, this is what I get; I just complete the ultimate sacrifice, and I get that."

"Take what you can get," Valor said, snorting, "Where's Nightsky?"

"Um," Rose said, looking around, "she's over there with Nightmare and Vengeance; looks as though they are coming this way."

James, Rose, and Valor all waited for the other three to join them.

"What's wrong?" Rose said, noting the less-than-pleased look on Vengeance's face. Rose couldn't help but feel somewhat satisfied by her disgust.

"Jonathan and Constance bolted after they saw you topple Igneous," Nightmare said as he limped forward.

"Cowards," Nightsky snorted, shaking her mane and shuffling her wings.

"Yes, it is rather depressing," Vengeance groaned and examined a wound on her leg.

"Well," Rose said, placing one hand on her hip, "we will just have to deal with them when they decide to make problems with us."

"We'll see,"Vengeance whispered and looked at Nightmare in a mysterious way.

"You are so cute, Rose," James laughed.

"Really?" Rose said, giving him a shy look and slapping him in the arm.

"Ouch!" he said, grinning and continuing to laugh.

"Come, Rose," Nightsky said and knelt down so Rose could get on. "We need to show the world that the war is over and a new regime has begun."

"Can James ride with me?"

"Yes."

Carefully, Rose and James sat on Nightsky's back, and with a flash of brilliant light, Rose and he were clad in her family's armor. The room began to change. Banners fluttered as if a wind had caught them. Their reds were replaced with every variation of green. The ceiling turned from a painted black dome to an all-glass one to show a sky filled with a new dawn. The pillars were covered with vines that were flowering as she sat there.

"Ready?" Nightsky asked as she stood up, swishing her tail.

"Ready," they replied.

Rose felt a jolt just above her navel as Nightsky took off. She flew down the hallway and into the entrance hall. As she flew, the changes that took place in the throne room followed them, and life began to spring back into the castle.

The pillars turned into while marble, and the banisters were a rich and polished rosewood. Windows were thrown open. Pots and vases, filled with every kind of rose imaginable and of every color, filled every room.

Gone were the terrible decorations depicting torture and pain; life replaced them. Paintings that once depicted the horrible king now depicted the planet's heritage, Rose's family crest, and paintings of her ancestors.

Nightsky flew out into the courtyard, and Rose watched as the last of the fighting stopped and as most of the soldiers began to surrender or pledge allegiance to the new order. They all watched in awe as the new ruler of Aquamarine flew overhead. Sun now filled the land, coming up from the east and warming the tired souls below. The brilliant rays were sending any remaining creatures of darkness into the Mountains of Treachery and beyond.

"This is so amazing!" James whispered into her ear as they continued to fly over the city and over its gates. They watched as the tired fields of brown turned greener than Rose could have imagined.

"Turning about," Nightsky warned, and she turned to go back over the city walls. She was now flying toward the castle, which was now flying flags with the Heartington crest in colors of blue, purple, and green.

She flew over the castle and circled around a terrible-looking garden before slowly descending into it. The terrible garden they lay in looked as though death himself might have been planted there.

"Eh," James said, making a disgusted face as he looked around and then reached up to lower Rose to the ground.

But the minute her foot touched the ground, the derelict earth beneath their feet began to shake. There was a deep rumble, and it seemed to be coming from beneath them.

"What's happening!" Rose cried over the noise.

"The world is righting itself!" Nightsky cried out to them.

Rose turned and suddenly saw a rock that looked strangely similar. It looked just as the one she had seen in the room belowground. The one in the room of roses.

"Over here!" she called and pulled James with her as the ground smelled of fresh earth and parts began to turn green.

"Why here!?" he asked over the rumble.

"Because," she said even more loudly, "this is the only piece of ground that isn't moving; look."

He and Nightsky looked down, and they all watched as every rose bush she had seen bloom below began rising from the earth. They were as bubbles that came to the surface of a boiling lake, as though the earth itself was the water.

"Amazing," Rose whispered in awe.

Then, as suddenly as the earth had begun to move, it once more returned to its solid state. And as the sun came over the ridge, it was like they were sitting in a bejeweled crown. The area simply sparkled in the prism of gems.

"Rose!" James exclaimed in excitement as he walked hurriedly over to the first bush he saw, "Rose! These are the bushes from the story!"

"Yah," Rose said, joining him by the bush that was blooming roses of pure diamond. "I guess I was wrong about you."

"Say what!" he said, looking at her in a hurt way.

"You can't tell a good story to save your life," she said, smiling.

"Oh that's it," he smiled, grabbing her waist and kissing her.

"Now, what were you saying?" he asked as they stopped for a moment.

"I think I meant you were off to a good start." She smiled. She then wrapped her arms around his neck while craning her own to kiss him again.

"Your Highness."

It was Don and Aphra, and they were running toward them.

"Don! Aphra!" Rose cried and ran to hug them both. She even hugged Courage and Siren. "I'm so glad to see you are both all right."

"Well," Aphra said, a wry smile on her face, "so are we, and since Dad's gone, we wanted to ask you two for your blessing."

"Oh, that's wonderful!" Rose cried out in joy, hugging them both again. "Of course you have it."

"Good for you, brother." James said, grinning, "Now you can stop eyeing my girl."

"Rose."

It was Nightsky, and she was looking in the direction of the door leading back into the castle, where there were men now standing.

"Yes?" Rose called in their direction.

"Your Highness," one said, bowing and coming before her, "they need you in the throne room."

"OK," she said breathlessly.

As she walked back behind the man, she was completely amazed by the castle's transformation. It was so much brighter, and it smelled of roses and fresh air.

Once in the throne room, a sad sight filled her eyes. Many people now lay in peaceful positions, and animals were positioned in much the same way. In the center was Topaz, with Thomas gracefully lying beside her. It was hard to see those she had known killed in a battle so brutally.

"Oh, James," Rose said, tears filling her eyes.

One by one Rose paid her respects to those who had fallen in order for her to succeed. Some she had known well but not by name, and some she had never met. She had left James standing with Don and Aphra, beside Topaz. They stayed there until those in charge of her grave came to retrieve her.

"Don," Aphra whispered softly, "she would have wanted it to be this way. She couldn't have lived without Evan."

Don nodded and placed a hand on James's shoulder. Rose learned later that day that no one had found a body that belonged to Evan Dugrin, and Vengeance had disappeared as well. Many believed that they may have run after Jonathan and Constance, but none knew for sure. Their animals, Nightmare and Allegiance, had disappeared, it seemed, along with them.

After all the individuals were buried, a monument was erected near the river, a little ways from the city walls. It was a depiction of the battle that took place and was built in remembrance of those who had given their lives on that day. Rose even planted two of the rose bushes at its base so that people would always remember.

Each of the deceased received a special marble headstone with a gem set in it. The gem served as a reminder that they had fought and died in the Battle of Emerald Thorns on Aquamarine.

Rose requested that the planet participate in a day of mourning after the last person was buried.

Constance and Jonathan were moving quickly toward a door in the basement of Stipes' summer home.

"I sure hope you're right, Constance, about them taking us back," Jonathan breathed as he wrenched open a door that had been made out of Tungsten metal and revealed a completely alternate world. "Because if they don't, Evan and Vengeance are going to get ahold of us, and trust me: you don't want that."

"Why should they?" Constance said, slyly leaping in before him, "Who's going to provide an alternate story?"

"I'm just saying, Devlon and Donevon Magus don't like to be lied to and know when the have been"

"Well they'll have no way of proving it, and if I were you, I'd be more worried about your wife, Citrine." Constance hissed, getting annoyed and moving forward.

"Why did you have to bring her up?" he moaned. And shaking his head, he snapped his fingers, and a fire started in the basement. Then he entered the other world, and taking what he thought would be a final look at Aquamarine, he closed the door, allowing the home to become a ruin of its own.

CHAPTER 37

The New Beginning

After the day of mourning, life on the planet began to resume, and Rose's coronation was organized. It was done on a beautiful day, with the sun shining overhead. She decided that the best way to make peace in the kingdom was to invite everyone to the coronation. The end result was a full castle, courtyard, and city. Once crowned, she knighted the original group, or all that remained of it, that came to Earth to retrieve her.

Sometime after, Liam and Rachel got married and had Rose do the honors; they are now expecting a child and hope it to be a boy, as they already have a name: Danny Draughtningr.

Vengeance and Evan were never found, but Rose suspected that they hadn't died but rather had disappeared. Perhaps there were other worlds they didn't know about yet.

Aphra and Don got hitched not long after Liam and Rachel did, and they happily ran a farm and started to rebuild Tungsten Manor. They decided to leave Draughtningr Manor to Liam and Rachel. Liam told his sister that he would do his best to return the home to its former glory.

Poor Pricilla passed away of a stroke shortly after the coronation. Some say it was caused by heartbreak, having lost her son. Her Cocker Spaniel, Aurora, now lives with Marina and Comis, and they work in the castle as the keepers of the library for Rose.

Rose, once she was crowned, agreed to be James's girlfriend once more, although she was sure that he had hoped she would want to marry him. She did love him, but there were things to do, and she didn't have time to give marriage the proper consideration. Things were looking up for the people and creatures of Aquamarine. That is, for now.

Index

Characters in A Tiara of Emerald Thorns

Rose Heartington: Daughter of Nicholas V and Diane Heartington. Keeper of the Tiara of Emerald Thorns. She is the girlfriend of James Tungston. Unicorn's name: **Nightsky**. She is a black-winged unicorn.

Tungston:

Neil Tungston: Father of James, Don, and Topaz Tungston. Son of Rita and Charlie Tungston. Husband of Silvia Tungston. Wife is deceased. A white dog named **Regal**.

Don Tungston: Oldest child of Neil and Silvia Tungston. Brother of younger siblings, Topaz and James Tungston. Black Hippogriff named **Courage**.

Topaz Tungston: Middle child of Neil and Silvia Tungston. Sister to older brother, Don Tungston and younger brother, James Tungston. Golden raven named **Thomas**.

James Tungston: Youngest child of Neil and Silvia Tungston. Younger brother to Don and Topaz Tungston. Boyfriend of Rose Heartington. The head of training for RTET and a skilled fighter. Black horse with emerald streaks named **Valor**.

Draughtningr:

Devin Draughtningr: Father of Liam and Aphra Draughtningr. Husband of Elizabeth Draughtningr. Second-in-command of RTET and has a white lizard named **Orpheus**. Wife is deceased.

Liam Draughtningr: Son of Devin and Elizabeth Draughtningr. Older brother of Aphra Draughtningr. Head of weapons division (RTET). Gray wolf named **Enigma**.

Aphra Draughtningr: Daughter of Devin and Elizabeth Draughtningr. Younger sister of Liam Draughtningr. Head of the Cryptic Conspirators (RTET): they are hidden in the king's most important areas, gathering critical information for their cause. A sapphire fox named **Siren**.

Griffen:

Marina Griffen: Daughter of Pricilla and Brian Griffen. Older sister to Dathen Griffen. A maid for the Draughtningrs. A crimson Cocker Spaniel named **Comis**.

Pricilla Griffen: Wife of Brian Griffen. Mother of Marina and Dathen Griffen. A maid for the Draughtningrs. A black and gold Cocker Spaniel named **Aurora**. Husband deceased.

Dathen Griffen: Son of Pricilla and Brian Griffen. Younger brother of Marina Griffen. Male servant for the Draughtningrs. A silver Cocker Spaniel named **Proditor**.

Dugrin:

Evan Dugrin: Son of Derik and Yvette Dugrin, older brother of Vengeance Dugrin. Head of all RTET sections, including the Cryptic Conspirators and the lower level of spies called Thorns. An all-black tiger by the name of **Allegiance** is his only true companion.

Vengeance Dugrin: Daughter of Derik and Yvette Dugrin, younger sister of Evan Dugrin. She is head of security for all members of RTET and is the head of Thorns, the lower-level spy operation. A gray and white hippogriff by the name of **Nightmare** is more loyal to her than she believes any man could be.

MacNeil:

Danny MacNeil: Son of Levi and Flora MacNeil, both deceased. Older brother of Rachel MacNeil. He is a member of Thorns and was working on becoming a Cryptic Conspirator. A red snake named **Tormen** was the animal that chose him.

Rachel MacNeil: Daughter of Levi and Flora MacNeil, both deceased. Younger sister of Danny MacNeil. A Cryptic Conspirator under the guise of a maid for the king. A white cat named **Damien** is the animal that chose her.

Villains:

Igneous Stipes: Father and mother unknown. Origins unknown. Sorcerer and current king/dictator of Aquamarine. Brother of Jonathan Stipes. Controller of the army, Annihilation, and murderer of Joseph Heartington and his son, Nicholas Heartington. Animal: gray-ash horse named **Infestus**.

Exotius Obscurum: Leader of the army of Annihilation and murderer of many. Origins are unknown. Human: maybe. Family: none. Animal: bloodred horse with a black tail and mane named **Wildfire**.

Jonathan Stipes: Parents unknown. Origins unknown. Brother of the king, Igneous Stipes. Animal: white leopard with red spots named **Constance**.

Impassive:

Jasmine Traymeda: Origins unknown. Family unknown. Age: Old. Animal: Calico in color, a white, gold, and black, cat named **Indifferens.**

Creatures

Puggles: animals with long, thin faces that have no mouth, only a small hole that sucks on any blood-bearing creature. No bigger than five centimeters and has a small, thin body that makes it slither like a snake. Can be spiked if it is angry or preparing to mate.

Note: Spikes are poisonous to humans but provide an antidote to their own poison if it is derived properly.

Trasicores (pronounced *tras-ih-coars*): animals with two tentacles, six legs, two arms, and two fangs. It has two mouths but one tongue that is used for both, as it can be up to a foot in length and is able to move up and down the single throat that leads to two stomachs. Tongues are very valuable, as they provide the essential ingredient for many poisons and antidotes. Getting a tongue is difficult, as the beast can be up to twenty feet tall. It has four pairs of eyes, two on its face and two on the back of its head, and can choose to use either pair or both at the same time. Only 50 around. **It is endangered and is kept as a pet by the king, used for executions. Preferred meals: humans or frogs, but eat all forms of mammals.**

Note: It has a hard time figuring out which limb to use to grab its meal, making it exceedingly clumsy and a hazard to itself as much as it is to its intended meal.

Froakes (pronounced (*frow-aches*): an amphibian that came to pass when snakes escaped through the portal between Earth and Aquamarine and one mated with a Frow.

Note: The snakes that already existed on Aquamarine could only be found in small numbers in the Forest of Promise and were created in the same manner as all of the creatures found there. How they are created is unknown to the people of Aquamarine.

These strange creatures do not like water except for laying their eggs or dying. They have a snakelike body with wings like a Frow and still prefer fruit as a food, which they swallow like a snake would. They have become a favorite food of Puggles due to their inability to move quickly.

Frow: Frog-like creature that has wings, webbed feet, and gills that allows it to dwell on land and in water. Living off of fruit-bearing trees, it does most of its feeding out of water and sleeps mostly in it. It lays eggs in the same manner that an Earth frog does; however, they hatch fully capable of flight and with self-sufficient knowledge of how to care for themselves.

Word Meanings

Fiery Branch ----------------------------------- Igneous Stipes

Beautiful Kingdom of Thorns ------------------ Decorus Regnum Corset

Dangerously ----------------------------------- Infestus

Kind --- Comis

Traitor--- Proditor

Pretty--- Siren

Mystery --------------------------------------- Enigma

Luminis --------------------------------------- Light

Veteris Spiritus ------------------------------- Ancient Spirits

Smaragaid ------------------------------------- Emerald

Aquamarine Words / Names

* Draughtningr ------------------------------- Quick Blade
(drot-ning-gr)
* Traymeda ------------------------------------ Fair Fortune
(tray-me-da)
* Touringrin ------------------------------------ Tall Trees
(toor-in-grin)
* Mourif ------------------------------------- Mountain Valley
(moor-iff)
* Coarif --------------------------------------- Courage
(coar-iff)
* Farrenlin ------------------------------------- Fair Life
(fair-ren-lin)
* Veteris Ferigan Magus----------------------- Ancient Forgotten Magic
* Spirorahd Eontach --------------------------- Of Great Spirit

Made in the USA
Las Vegas, NV
11 June 2021